BOOKS BY MARY ANDERSON

MATILDA INVESTIGATES

I'M NOBODY! WHO ARE YOU?

JUST THE TWO OF THEM

EMMA'S SEARCH FOR SOMETHING

F.T.C. SUPERSTAR!

MATILDA'S MASTERPIECE

MATILDA'S MASTERPIECE

Mary Anderson

ILLUSTRATED BY SAL MURDOCCA

Atheneum   New York

1977

Library of Congress Cataloging in Publication Data
Anderson, Mary, *Matilda's masterpiece.*
Summary: *When she practically witnesses the theft of
a valuable painting, twelve-year-old Mattie
does her own detective work to
trap the thief.*
[1. *Mystery and detective stories*]   *I. Murdocca,
Sal. II. Title.*
PZ7.A5444Mav   [Fic]   76-40981
ISBN 0-689-30565-6

TO INGEBORG
our "sophisticated" aunt . . . a true original!

MATILDA'S
MASTERPIECE

CHAPTER

1

"I still can't believe she's dead," Mattie brooded, throwing her magazine on the kitchen floor. "The great voice of Agatha Christie, silenced forever."

"Quick, get the paper towels," said Jonathon excitedly.

"Don't worry," she assured him, "I'm not going to cry again. I've had months to recover from shock. The great old lady's gone!"

"The towels aren't for *you*," he groaned, lifting the hot frying pan from the stove. "They're for the bacon. Dad likes his crisp and dry."

But Mattie didn't hear him.

"It was bad enough losing Hercule Poirot in that

last book," she sighed. "But he was a *man*."

Jonathon took a loaf of white bread from the counter. "And Agatha was an old lady," he said matter-of-factly. "When people get real old, they die. You don't have to be a detective to figure that out."

"You don't understand," snapped Mattie, grabbing a strip of bacon. "When Dame Agatha died, Miss Marple died with her. One of the world's few female detectives, dead as a doornail!"

Jonathon shook his head and began dipping the bread in his egg batter. "I saw a Miss Marple movie once," he said, dropping each slice into the sizzling pan. "She was awful old, too."

"What a blow to Woman's Lib," Mattie muttered.

Jonathon paused and looked thoughtful. "Think I should've made sausages instead of bacon? Or waffles instead of French toast?"

"What a great old gal she was. Someone a young, intelligent, female detective could look up to!"

"I want everything to go right while old Bascomb's away," he said, flipping each slice. "I've got to convince Daddy we don't need a housekeeper anymore. I cook and clean better anyway; always have."

"Maybe she had some more books stashed away in her vault," sighed Mattie wistfully.

Jonathon checked the clock and began setting the table. "Daddy's got five more minutes to sleep. Everything should go like clockwork." Taking three glasses from the kitchen cabinet, he paused again. "Tomato or orange juice?"

"Being a detective's hard enough," Mattie continued. "I *need* my idols to look up to. You've got Betty Crocker, but who've I got?"

"Tomato." Jonathon smiled. "With just a squirt of lemon juice. What do you think, Mattie? Should I put lemon in it?"

"What do I care?" she answered, pushing open the kitchen door and pounding into the living room. "Shove a sock in it!"

"What's all the racket?" asked Mr. Cosgrave, rubbing his eyes and yawning. "Breakfast ready yet?"

"Not yet," said Mattie, throwing herself on the sofa. "Jonathon hasn't finished putting panties on the bacon slices."

"Oh, another of *those* mornings?" He sighed. "Think I'll go shave."

"Was that Daddy?" asked Jonathon, poking the kitchen door open with his spatula. "French toast'll be finished in a minute. I've cut some cantaloupe. Think Daddy wants cantaloupe?"

"Afraid not. He just smelled your breakfast. He's in the bathroom, throwing up."

Jonathon stuck his tongue out, then closed the kitchen door. Mattie tried to pay no attention. Talking with Jonathon was always unsatisfying and usually unnerving. He had such an unsympathetic attitude toward matters that didn't interest him. Cooking and cleaning were his favorite topics. If you couldn't fry it, broil it or wax it, he wouldn't discuss it.

As she sat, her chin scrunched up into her knees, she noticed a white towel slowly drifting onto her lap. Then she felt her father's hands gently grab her by the shoulders.

"What's this for?" she asked, glancing up at him.

Mr. Cosgrave had washed, shaved and dressed. He was wearing his tan corduroy jacket with the brown leather elbow patches (exactly what Mattie felt a big New York reporter should always wear).

"Flag of truce?" he asked. "Between you and Jonathon; just long enough for us to eat breakfast."

Mattie smiled. What a super Dad, always knowing when something bothered her. Having only one parent wasn't so bad when he was a terrific one.

"All right, everyone be seated," called Jonathon from the kitchen.

"Aren't you gonna ring a crystal bell and wear white gloves?"

"Matilda," said her father firmly, pulling out her chair. "Truce." He glanced over the table. "Wouldn't Miss Bascomb be pleased with you!" He smiled, spreading his paper napkin onto his lap. "Everything looks wonderful, son."

"Gosh, I should've used the linen napkins," Jonathon groaned.

"What's the fuss about?" asked Mattie, digging into her cantalope. "You've cooked at least a thousand meals. What's so special about this morning?"

"You do seem nervous," his father observed. "*Is* this morning special?"

"Yes, Daddy," he said haltingly. "I'm applying for a job today."

"Jobs are hard to get lately, especially for ten-year-old boys. What is it, delivering groceries? You know I don't like you going inside strange buildings."

"It's in *this* building, Daddy. In this apartment. I'm applying for old Bascomb's housekeeping job."

"*Miss* Bascomb," he corrected. "And she's only gone to visit her sister in Ossining for a week or ten days, Jonathon—not *forever*. A temporary agency can send someone until she comes back."

"That's what I'm applying for," he explained. "I'm perfect for the job. I know the layout, and I cook and clean much better than old Bascomb. Besides, I'll need the experience for my résumé someday."

"When your mother died, Miss Bascomb became part of our household," Mr. Cosgrave explained. "She's cared for you kids ever since. She's almost one of the family."

"Well, we don't have to *dump* her. Just let me run the place while she's away. I've been waiting for a chance like this," he pleaded. "I'll do all the shopping, too. We don't need to hire anyone else. Besides, I'll work real cheap."

"A point in your favor," said his father. "And I do like your initiative. Okay, as long as you have time for your schoolwork, too. Let's say fifteen dollars for the week, plus our charge account at the supermarket?"

"Terrific!" Jonathon shouted. "I'll do a great job, Daddy. This place'll be shining when old Bascomb returns. And I'll save you money, too. I've got a big list of budget menus I'm dying to try. Bascomb doesn't shop too well, you know. While she gabs with the vegetable man, he sneaks wilted lettuce and bruised apples into her cart. She's not great on dustballs, either. There're some real tumbleweeds under the sofa."

"Good Lord," Mattie groaned. "Can't we discuss some *serious* matters for a change?"

"Of course," said her father. "What's on your mind?"

"The same old stuff," teased Jonathon. "Mattie read another article about Agatha Christie this morning and flipped out again."

"See what I mean, Dad," said Mattie angrily. "No one takes me seriously. This house is *crawling* with discrimination. Listen to how Jonathon talks about dear Miss Bascomb behind her back."

Jonathon choked on his cantaloupe. "*Me?* You call her Hatchet Face and Dracula's Daughter!"

"Never mind," said Mattie. "I'm tired of everyone thinking I'm a weirdo just because I want to devote my life to crime detection. Someday, the name Ma-

tilda Cosgrave will be as famous as Sherlock Holmes and Miss Marple."

"Right," giggled Jonathon. "They're both unreal, and so are you."

"You ungrateful brat," she shouted, her face reddening. "That's not what you said last week when I figured out who stole your homework."

"Quite true," her father agreed. "You've solved a lot of puzzling problems, Mattie. And I'm sorry you feel misunderstood. But be reasonable. Not many twelve-year-old girls *want* to be private detectives. It takes some getting used to. I don't fully accept it, myself."

"Oh, Dad," she groaned.

"Really," he added. "I've never liked the idea of your sneaking around looking for crimes and crooks. Goodness knows, they're easy enough to find in this neighborhood. Broadway's crawling with junkies and winos; back seats of stolen cars filled with ripped-off goods. It's not a healthy atmosphere for a young girl."

"I agree, Dad. Second-rate crimes are gross; not my style at all. I'm through solving petty crimes. I'm experienced enough now for some classy crimes. A bank robbery or a diamond theft!"

Mr. Cosgrave quickly swallowed his last gulp of coffee. "I hope you're being overly dramatic, Matilda."

"Honest," she argued. "I'm ready for the big stuff —crooks who wear tuxedos instead of stockings on their faces. The world of jewel thieves and stolen yachts."

"Crooks are crooks," said Jonathon flatly. "And they'd have to be *limping* for you to catch them."

"You're getting your values a little mixed, honey," her father frowned. "All crooks break the law, well-dressed or not. And I'd prefer that you stayed away from both types."

"It's not fair," she pouted. "Jono gets a chance to do *his* thing. You're even paying him for it. What do I get? Nothing!"

"Jonathon lucked into an opportune situation. He was ambitious enough to take advantage of it. I couldn't refuse."

"But what about me?" she insisted. "I've got equal rights."

"All right, Mattie." He sighed. "So you have. If, at school today, you come across any high-class crimes —jewel thieves or yacht robbers—you have my personal permission to investigate them. Word of honor."

Mattie grit her teeth. "That's not funny, Dad."

"But fair," he added. "I've got to go, kids. I'm interviewing a mayoral assistant at nine thirty. Have a good day. See you tonight."

"What would you like for dinner?" asked Jonathon. "My new recipe for roast chicken or hamburger bundles?"

"Surprise me. But stick to our budget. Bye, kids."

When Mattie was certain their father had gone, she

turned to Jonathon. "What would you like for dinner, daddy-dearie? Heart of hamburger?" She tossed the cantaloupe rind in his direction. "You big meatball!"

"Jealousy is self-destructive," he said haughtily. "And counter-productive," he added, clearing away the dishes.

"Real catchy saying, Confucius. Find it in a fortune cookie?"

"That reminds me," he said, taking a bag from the refrigerator. "There's no cookies, so I put an orange in your lunch. I toasted the bread to take the sog out and included some carrot sticks."

Mattie grabbed the bag and walked away. How disgustingly humiliating, how ego-deflating, how *unbearable* to have a brother so well organized.

"Hey, wait for me," he called. "Once I've rinsed these dishes, I'm finished."

"Tough. I can't afford to be late for school today. We're going on a class trip."

"You can't afford to be late any day. Not with your rotten marks."

"They teach the wrong things," she argued. "No crime detection, no fingerprinting or criminal psychology. They should have ballistic tests instead of math tests."

"Quit sulking." He laughed. "Your big chance has finally come. Remember Daddy's promise. If you see a major crime in school today, you've got his permission to solve it."

Mattie stamped toward the front door. "Confucius say: Boy who make rotten remark, get ice cube in his bunk tonight and cockroach in his breakfast tomorrow." Slamming the door loudly, she buzzed for the elevator.

CHAPTER

2

When Mattie got to school, her class was in more than its usual state of confusion. Everyone was trying to find out where Mrs. Almquist was taking them on their "surprise" class trip. Mattie hoped it wouldn't be the zoo again. Whenever she had nowhere else to go, Mrs. Almquist dragged kids to the zoo. However, when Mattie heard that they were going to the Brooklyn Museum, she wasn't sure that was much better.

Everybody was given a partner and then hustled into a straight line. To Mattie's disgust, her buddy for the day turned out to be Melissa Remington, one of her least favorite people. Melissa was a gorgeous, clever, fragile thing, who never burped or had a pimple. Her socks never rolled down, and her hair never got mussed. Even worse, she disliked Mattie, but adored Jonathon. Mattie was sure she only pretended to like Jono for spite, knowing it made her skin crawl.

"Guess we're to spend the day together." Melissa smiled.

"Be still my heart," Mattie mumbled.

"Some people don't deserve a cultural experience," Melissa answered, tossing her shiny curls over her shoulders with a silky bounce.

"Ain't it the truth."

Mrs. Almquist smiled and ushered the children from the classroom, up to Broadway and into the Seventh Avenue Subway. It was a long ride to Brooklyn. The boys began punching one another, while the girls tried to talk above the noise of the subway. Mattie wished she'd brought a good detective novel!

In spite of Mattie's icy glances, Melissa kept trying to start a conversation. "It's too bad Jonathon isn't along," she cooed. "He's so creative, he'd appreciate a trip like this. My mother says he'd make a great interior decorator."

Was that an insult? Interior decorators were supposed to be "strange." Jono was a fat little neatsy-poo pest, but he wasn't "strange."

"In olden days," Melissa continued, "talented people had patrons who guided their careers. Poor, struggling artists became protégés of the rich."

Another dig? Embarrassed, Mattie glanced at her

worn-down shoes. Melissa probably washed her face with dollar bills!

"All right," Mrs. Almquist announced, "at the next stop, take your buddy's hand and leave the train in an orderly fashion."

Mattie stood up, refusing Melissa's hand. The class piled out at the Eastern Parkway station. Mattie had never seen the Brooklyn Museum before, but it looked like the Metropolitan, which she'd been to many times. (Jonathon liked to drag her through the eighteenth and nineteenth century rooms, commenting on the decor.) It seemed as large as the Metropolitan; a big gray stone building that covered several blocks.

There were five floors inside, and the class couldn't decide which to go to first. Some voted for costumes and period rooms; others the Egyptian collection and paintings. Mrs. Almquist promised they'd try to see everything.

The morning was spent looking at Pre-Columbian and Indian art, the Hall of the Americans and the Plains Indians, and fifteenth century drawings and woodcuts. In the Egyptian wing, they passed cases of pottery and sculpture. In the Costume Gallery they saw displays of fashion through the ages.

Most of the kids found the tour fun. But to Mattie, museums always seemed dull. She'd always thought of them as art supermarkets, filled with too many dead things. Melissa had been right, though, it was exactly the type of trip Jonathon would have adored. He could've gotten lost for hours in the details of one Chinese urn. On their trips to the Metropolitan, Jonathon would rattle on forever about the delicate work in a tapestry or the subtle veneer of a table. Nauseating!

By noon, Mattie was grateful for the lunch break in the cafeteria. She had to listen to Melissa jabber, but at least her feet and eyes got a rest. After lunch, the class wandered through the Gallery Shop, looking at the things on sale. There were hand-carved masks and toys, and handicrafts and jewelry from all over the world. Mattie noticed a magnifying glass from Germany just perfect for her collection. She bought it and tucked it in her purse. When everyone had had a chance to buy something, the class was herded to the fifth floor to view American and French Impressionist paintings.

By now, Mattie knew she'd had enough culture for one day, so sat down on a sofa in the center gallery. Melissa reappeared and "buddied" herself down there, too.

"I've been giving your brother's problem a lot of thought all day," she whispered.

"Which problem? He's got so many."

"His creativity's being stifled," she explained. "He's such a marvelous cook and housekeeper. You, on the other hand, are only interested in *criminal* elements. He must suffer. But my mother appreciates artistic people. She was once chairman of . . ."

17

Mattie tuned out and began staring at a painting on the opposite wall. It was the first thing she'd seen all day she really liked. The small pastel in shades of brown and beige showed a young girl in a large straw hat with an impish, mysterious grin. Her eyes held a pleasant twinkle, lit by a warm, friendly glow. Seeing something strangely familiar in the portrait, Mattie lost herself in the girl's expression. She could almost hear her speak; a thin, old-fashioned voice, muffled under lace. She stared at the picture a long time.

"This is preposterous!" someone shouted. "It's *illegal*."

Mattie blinked and turned around. At the far end of the gallery, an old woman was trying to leave. A guard blocked her way.

"I never heard of such a thing," she shouted. "By whose authority are you doing this?"

"Sorry, ma'am," said the guard, holding his ground. "I've got orders. No one leaves the gallery for the next few minutes."

"What's the trouble?" asked Mrs. Almquist nervously. "I was about to take my class back to school. I hope this isn't—"

"Don't know what it is, ma'am," he answered blankly. "I've got to hold everyone here awhile. Orders from my chief."

"All right." She sighed, gathering up the class and herding them toward a corner. "There are several fascinating pictures we haven't seen yet."

"What's the matter?" asked Jimmy Folsum. "Won't they let us leave?"

"Na," teased Willard. "We're their prisoners. That's how they get dummies for those costumes downstairs. They're gonna dip us all in wax, then dress us up funny."

A second guard ran into the gallery, frantically poking behind chairs and pulling something from under the sofa.

"I bet there's been a *bomb scare!*" said Adam. "This place is gonna blow sky high."

"That's stupid," said Mattie. "They don't keep people *in* buildings with bombs, they get them *out*."

"Then maybe someone stole something," said Christina.

"How could they?" Melissa laughed. "We've got the class *detective* with us. Nothing gets past her beady eyes."

"It's merely a mix-up," said Mrs. Almquist reassuringly. "We'll be out in a moment. Meanwhile, this Cezanne . . ."

By now, several persons had tried leaving the gallery, but all had been refused. At first, they seemed surprised and went off to wait quietly. But after twenty minutes, Mrs. Almquist was nervous, and the other visitors were really upset.

"Can't you at least tell us *why*?" one insisted.

"The director will be here soon," announced the guard. "He'll explain."

The director? Maybe there *had* been a robbery! Excitedly, Mattie glanced around the gallery. What had been unimportant visitors now suddenly became potential suspects in a major crime. She began staring at the faces around her. The portrait had been interesting, but *real* faces were far better. People's eyes and expressions told countless stories; when she really looked at people, she always felt as if she were crawling inside them, unearthing their secrets. Systemically, Mattie noted each adult in the gallery.

There were eight of them, besides Mrs. Almquist. Most of them had begun speaking with one another; asking questions, shrugging shoulders, trying to extract further information from the guards. But one was different.

Mattie spied him almost at once, an old man who had set himself apart from the others. He stood hunched in a corner, as if he wanted to blend into the wall. He was a short man in his sixties, wearing rundown, scruffy shoes and a soiled raincoat. A beat-up felt hat threw sinister shadows across a face etched with lines.

Noticing her staring, the old man glanced at her menacingly. Mattie peered through the shadows into the cloudy grayness of his eyes, startled at what she saw there. They were eyes filled with fear and apprehension. Mattie had seen eyes like that once before, but couldn't remember where. It almost scared her to look into them.

Suddenly realizing how long she had been staring, Mattie turned away. As she did, the old man began pacing the room nervously, his head darting back and forth like a frantic caged bird. A definite criminal type, obviously planning his escape.

Escape from *what*? That was still a mystery! Several more minutes passed before the museum's director came in, escorted by two police officers. The policemen and guard stood by the exit, blocking the doorway.

"My name is Mr. Butterick," he announced somberly. "I'm sorry for this inconvenience."

"What's going on?" asked a man. "I've got a train to catch."

"You can't lock people into your building," an old lady protested.

The old man said nothing. He continued fidgeting nervously and glancing toward the exit.

"There's been a robbery," Mr. Butterick announced. "One of our Degas paintings was taken from the adjoining gallery. Museum officials are locking all the exits. I'm afraid you must all remain in the building until the police have taken your names and addresses. Unfortunately, you must also be searched."

"No one's searching me!" said one woman. "I haven't stolen anything."

"Are you sure it's been stolen?" someone asked. "Maybe someone took it down to clean."

"I'm afraid not," said Mr. Butterick. "The two

wires that held the painting remain on the wall. The frame was found minutes ago under that green sofa in this very gallery. I've checked with everyone. No staff member removed the painting for any reason."

"What'd you say was stolen?" asked the old lady.

"A Degas," Mr. Butterick repeated. "A small still life entitled *Seashells and Vegetables*. It's valued at over fifty thousand dollars."

The visitors turned to each other again.

"Fifty thousand. Holy cow!"

"I noticed that empty space, but never thought . . ."

"No sense holding us. The thief's miles away by now."

"The mayor's to blame for this. Imagine, searching me!"

"Personally, I'm not afraid to be searched."

At the mention of being searched, Mattie noticed the old man's hands begin to shake. He riveted his eyes on the exit, as if immediate escape were a matter of life and death. Mattie was now certain she knew the whereabouts of the stolen painting; there was no other reason for his strange behavior.

"Please," Mr. Butterick interrupted. "We'll make you all as comfortable as possible. Chairs are on the way. I've asked to have some cards sent up from the gift shop for the children. If need be, we'll even have story hour."

"Story hour!" a man shouted. "Are you joking? I'm not staying for stories, or hours!"

"We've no choice, Fred," his wife cautioned. "The *police* are here."

"A story hour sounds sweet," said the old lady.

"My mother will be furious if I'm late," said Melissa.

Mattie could hardly believe her ears. How typical of Melissa to discuss mundane matters, while they were in the midst of a major crime. And why should the visitors grumble and complain over something so unbearably exciting. They'd practically all been eye-witnesses to a priceless art theft! Why, just moments before, Mattie herself had been seated on the sofa that had concealed the stolen painting's frame. Undoubtedly, the thief was still in this room. The short little man in the corner was obviously guilty. Why couldn't everyone *see* that? His sneaky expression, uneasy manner and nervous twitches were dead giveaways. He probably had the picture stuffed inside his dirty raincoat.

For a moment, Mattie had an irresistable urge to shout out, pointing an accusing finger. But as she glanced at the old man again, she felt strangely frightened. Besides, she had no real evidence, only a *feeling*. Good crime detection required *proof*, solid evidence that would stand up in court.

She could see herself in the crowded jury room now . . . twelve expressionless faces staring at her as she sat in the witness box . . . "Ms. Cosgrave," the defense attorney shouts threateningly, "on what basis do you charge this poor, dear man with the theft of a Degas?" "Yes," the judge joins in, "on what basis?" "It was his eyes, Your Honor," she answers sheepishly, "his cloudy gray eyes." The twelve members of the jury begin laughing hysterically, and the old man cackles gleefully . . .

"Certainly the *children* aren't confined here," Mrs. Almquist pleaded. "It's time I took them back to school."

"Maybe *you* clipped the picture, teacher," Adam said, laughing. "Then used the class as your cover. You *never* take us to the museum, always to the zoo."

"The building's been locked," said Mr. Butterick. "Everyone must remain. If you'll excuse me, I have to inform visitors in other galleries."

As Mr. Butterick left, a male and female officer entered to search the visitors.

Mrs. Almquist gasped. "You're not going to search the children!"

"No one's gonna frisk me," Eddie shouted.

The lady officer smiled. "We'll just take their names for our records."

With much poking, giggling and pushing, the class lined up. The confusion gave Mattie the chance she needed. She inched toward the opposite side of the room where another officer was taking the names of the other visitors. Discreetly, she slipped her notebook from her purse.

"I'm Emily Reardon, officer," said the old lady.

"What's your name, officer?"

Mattie watched as the little man deliberately positioned himself at the end of the line. When his turn came, hesitatingly, he gave his name. In a voice barely above a whisper, he stammered nervously through a thick European accent. "My name is Anton Milich. I live at 49 Delancey Street."

Quickly writing it down, Mattie stared at the old man again. She couldn't shake the feeling she'd seen him before. His frightened expression was definitely familiar. Maybe she'd seen his face on the FBI's Ten Most Wanted Criminals list! If only she were home, she could check her files.

When the officer began examining the old man's clothes, Mattie felt certain the stolen Degas would fall from his pockets. If only she'd spoken out earlier, she'd have received credit along with the Police Department.

What a headline! . . . "Anton Milich, a sneaky old man from Delancey Street was captured in the Brooklyn Museum today. Matilda Cosgrave, ardent feminist and crime detector, fingered the suspect just moments after he'd hidden a priceless Degas in his filthy raincoat . . ."

"All right, Mr. Milich," said the officer, finishing his search. "You may sit down."

Mattie's heart sank. He didn't have the painting after all! He must've ditched it somewhere in the building or passed it to an accomplice.

"Matilda, what's your address, dear?" asked Mrs. Almquist. "Officer Evans is waiting."

"Mattie's our personal private detective," teased Melissa. "She solves all the crimes in school; lost buttons, stolen pencils, missing grades."

"Really?" said Officer Evans, "You must be busy. Have any leads on this case? I'm sure the museum could use them."

"Yes, Mattie," said Melissa. "You were sitting right on the sofa where they found the picture frame. Didn't you *see* anyone?"

"No, I didn't."

"But the thief was right under your nose," said Adam.

"Under your *fanny*," said Melissa.

"It's nothing to joke about," Mrs. Almquist said.

"This whole thing's ridiculous," one visitor shouted. "How could someone walk off with a valuable painting?"

"It doesn't take long to undo a canvas," explained the policeman. "This place looks understaffed, and guards can't be everywhere at once."

"It's all these budget cuts," another groaned. "The city's falling apart!"

"But you can see none of us has the darn thing," the man added. "I don't even *like* Degas—too sentimental. Can't you let us go now?"

"Not until the entire building's been searched," said the guard firmly.

"I bet we've been here an hour already," one woman protested. "My cats will be hungry."

"Hey, Mattie," Adam shouted. "Tell the cops what you know so we can go."

"Does this girl know something?" asked the officer sharply.

"She knows *everything*," said Melissa slyly. "She was sitting right on that sofa when the thief dumped the frame."

"Don't conceal information," he cautioned.

"I don't know *anything*," Mattie protested.

Melissa laughed. "She finally confessed!" Poking Adam, she started a chain reaction of giggles through the class.

Mattie boiled. She'd make Melissa *eat* those words!

"I found some crayons in the gift shop," said a guard, coming in. "Maybe you kids want to use them while you wait?"

"Yeah," said Eddie. "Let's draw them another painting so they'll let us go."

"What's it called?" asked Christina.

"Seashells and Vegetables."

"Okay," she said, stretching out on the floor, "I'll draw the shells, you draw the vegetables."

"Children, *please*," Mrs. Almquist pleaded. "Try to cooperate.

"Sign it Degas." Christina giggled. "They'll never know."

Half an hour later, Mr. Butterick finally returned

to the gallery. "Our search is complete," he said wearily. "We've checked every package and parcel, every bathroom and stairway. The painting's nowhere to be found."

Bet they didn't check the plumbing, thought Mattie. Mr. Milich probably shoved it down a drain. If only she'd brought her pliers!

"The painting's definitely gone," he sighed. "We even checked the plumbing fixtures."

For the second time, Mattie's heart sank.

"Does that mean we can go now?" asked one man.

"Yes," said Mr. Butterick. "If the officer has your name and address, you may leave."

"Aren't we going to have story hour?" asked the old lady.

"Teachers and school children may use the office phones to contact parents. We're very sorry for any inconvenience this may have caused."

"Don't worry about it." Eddie grinned. "We made a new painting for you, mister. I put in lots of zucchini. And blue carrots. Christina stole my orange crayon."

Adam groaned. "Bet Mrs. Almquist makes us write some dumb composition about this whole dumb day."

"If you ask me," said Christina, *none* of these pictures is worth stealing. I like the sofa, though."

"Let's all have a reunion," Mrs. Reardon suggested. "We'll meet in this gallery every year on the anniversary of the theft. I'll bring the buns."

As Mr. Milich quickly exited, Mattie took a final look at her prime suspect. With no concrete evidence, she had to watch him go.

Mrs. Almquist led them to the elevator. "Children, this has been a most unusual day. Tonight, I want you all to write a composition about it."

"I missed violin practice," Amy moaned. "My mom'll kill me."

"Don't worry, class. We'll all go to the office and call home."

"Is your mom waiting, too, teacher?" Eddie laughed.

Mrs. Almquist sighed. "I wish she were. It's four thirty now, and it'll be another hour before we get back."

In the office, the children lined up to take turns using the telephones. There were only four, so it took time. It was almost five o'clock when Mattie finally reached Jonathon.

"Where have you been?" he shouted. "Wow, you're a fink, Mattie. You waltzed off this morning without making your bunk. There's toothpaste squooshed all over the sink. What's Dad gonna say? It's my responsibility to keep this house in order. I've spent an hour on dinner and don't have time to—"

"Shut your trap and listen," she interrupted. "I'm in the Brooklyn Museum."

"Well that's cute," he snapped. "You *never* want

to go to museums with me. But today, you trot all the way to Brooklyn, leaving me with piles of paste and wrinkled sheets."

"There's been a *robbery* here, pea brain. A priceless painting was ripped off a wall."

"Oh sure. And I bet you were there when it happened."

"Yes, and I'm still here. So's the whole class. We had to wait while the police searched the place."

"What a corny excuse. I'm not making your bed, no matter . . ."

"It's worth over fifty thousand dollars," she continued. "The place is crawling with cops. They even checked the plumbing. And listen, Jono, *I know who did it*! An old guy in a raincoat. The minute I saw him, I knew he was scared to death. But he's clever. The cops had to let him go for lack of evidence."

"Is this for real?"

"Of course. Listen, I'll be home in an hour and give you all the details. Isn't this great luck? An art thief dropped right in my lap. But I have to figure out where he hid the painting."

"That's sure a coincidence," Jonathon agreed. "Just this morning, Dad gave you permission and now you've got a case."

"What're you babbling about?"

"Don't you remember? Daddy said if you discovered a major crime today, he'd give you permission to solve it."

"Wow, I forgot!" she shouted. "If Dad remembers, I'm in big trouble."

"Why?"

"He only said that because he thought it was *impossible*. If I tell him what happened, he'll take back his promise. We've got to keep this *secret*."

"That's sneaky, Mattie."

"You bet. Now don't spill anything. Let's hope Dad forgot what he said. In a few days when I've got some clues, he won't mind so much."

"He's bound to find out," Jonathon argued. "He's a reporter. I'll bet it makes the front page."

"Gosh, I hadn't thought of that. Well, it's too late for today's paper. We'll keep him away from TV tonight, then steal his morning newspaper."

"Oh what a tangled web we weave, when first—"

"Leave the deception to me," she ordered. "Just keep quiet and do your kitchen bit."

"I made hamburger bundles," he said proudly. "They're in the oven now. But if you're not back by six o'clock, your bundle's going to be a lump."

"So's your head, if you don't keep your mouth shut."

"Blackmail, too, Mattie? *Tch-tch*! Listen, since you're at the Brooklyn Museum, why not pick us up some honey? It comes fresh from their apiary. I've got a great recipe for honey sticky-buns I'm dying to—"

Mattie slammed down the phone and sighed. She

checked her notebook, then placed Mr. Milich's address safely in her bag. Clinging to it tightly during the subway ride home made her feel assured. Things were looking great! She had a giant head start on the police. While they ran around checking phoney leads, she already knew the thief. The only mystery was where Mr. Milich had hidden the Degas. And though it might take time, she'd find out.

Mattie had made several studies of criminal behavior in general, but she realized she knew nothing about art thieves in particular. Before she could hope to trap Milich, she'd have to determine his M.O. That meant lots of research. She'd begin at the library tomorrow, right after school.

CHAPTER

3

Luck was on Mattie's side. She got home just minutes before her father, so there was no explaining to do. Jonathon's hamburger bundles popped from the oven bubbly and brown, so she hadn't messed up dinner. By the time they'd finished eating, the local news was over and her secret was still safe. There was only one touchy moment at dinner, when Jonathon brought in the apple crisp.

"Where'd you go on your class trip, Mattie?" asked Mr. Cosgrave. "The zoo again?"

Mattie was cool and evasive. "Not this time." Gulping down her dessert, she quickly changed the subject. "This stuff's terrific, Jono. What's in it?"

34

"One cup of apples sliced thin, three-fourths cup oatmeal mixed in one-half cup brown sugar. . . ."

After dinner, Mr. Cosgrave went into the study to write. He worked through the late news then went to bed. In the morning, he was still ignorant of the art theft and the fact that Mattie had actually been there when it happened.

Before breakfast, Mattie snatched the morning paper from the doormat. Quickly thumbing through, she read the major headlines. No mention of a theft. She'd begun looking at the smaller stories when her father passed.

"Thanks, honey," he said, taking the paper.

Oh well, she thought. Even if the robbery was mentioned, he'd never know she'd been there.

Mattie was even quieter at breakfast than she'd been at dinner. In her mind, a lovely fantasy kept playing itself out. . . .

. . . One morning soon, she'd enter the kitchen and dramatically drop the stolen painting on the table before her father's startled eyes. "Where'd you get this?" he'd gasp. "Oh father dear, didn't I tell you? I was in the museum the day this priceless Degas was stolen. Through clever deduction and tireless foot-work, I've trapped the sneaky old thief. Miss Marple may be dead, but we who are younger and stronger live on. . . ."

"How long is this going to continue, Matilda?" asked Mr. Cosgrave, peering over his newspaper.

"You can't fool me."

Jonathon turned green. "I didn't say a word," he whispered.

"No one has to tell me when something's wrong," he continued. "It's about yesterday, isn't it?"

"Yesterday?" asked Mattie innocently. "What about it?"

"You've been behaving strangely ever since. You wouldn't tell me about your class trip. And I'd almost forgotten . . ."

Mattie glared at her brother.

"I didn't tell him," he insisted.

"But now I know what to do about your problem," Mr. Cosgrave added, pointing to the paper. "Listen to this:

> *A Degas worth at least $50,000 disappeared yesterday from the Brooklyn Museum. Some 200 people were detained nearly two hours as museum officials locked all doors and the police searched all the visitors.*"

"Well," Mattie began feebly, prepared to confess all, "I was sitting on a sofa when this old lady started yelling. . . ."

"See the coincidence?" asked Mr. Cosgrave. "Only yesterday we discussed classy crimes, and here's one in the paper. This article's given me a great idea. Mattie, I've thought over our conversation yesterday, and you're right. You should have the same opportunities as Jonathon. Equal rights for all! This article might solve both our problems. My paper's given me a new assignment, and I want you to help me. It'll keep you out of trouble, earn you some money, and save me a lot of time."

"What're you talking about, Dad?"

"A new Sunday series for the paper. I'm writing six consecutive articles called psychological portraits. They're case studies of different types of people. I think now I'll include art thieves and forgers. It's a new slant, not done often. But each article requires lots of preparation. While Jonathon has his job running the house, I'd like to hire you for some crime research. Think you'd be interested?"

"You want *me* to solve this theft?"

Mr. Cosgrave laughed. "Of course not. The police'll do that. You go to the library and find out all you can about previous art thefts and forgeries. What type of person steals paintings? Why? Who does forgeries? How are forgeries detected? Are art thieves different from other thieves? Do museums have enough security? That sort of thing. Concentrate on the people and how they operate. I'll pay you the same salary Jonathon's getting. Fifteen dollars a week."

Mattie couldn't believe it. The exact kind of research she planned on her own, only now Dad had offered to *pay* for it! She was speechless.

"How about it? Sound fair?"

"Sure," she gulped. "I'll do a great job for you, Dad, honest."

"Oh yes," Jonathon sighed, "*honesty's* the best policy."

Ashamed, Mattie looked down at her plate. Her two fried eggs stared up accusingly. She was a deceitful, ungrateful, conniving child. Yet, it was too late to confess all about the museum trip and her hot suspect. Dad might take back his offer. He'd only given her the job to keep her *out* of trouble. Well, she'd make a solemn secret oath. If she got into any sticky situations while solving this art theft, she'd immediately call in the police.

"Now that we're all friends again," said Jonathon slyly, "Mattie can tell us about her swell class trip."

"Afraid I don't have time," said Mr. Cosgrave. "Got to run. Tell me about it later, okay, Mattie?"

"Sure, Dad. Much later."

"Hey, Mattie," Jonathon prodded. "You forgot to make your bunk again."

"I'll get to it."

"While you're at it, you can finish dusting, then wash the dishes. Water the plants, too. I won't have time."

"Those are *your* jobs," she protested. "Why should *I* do them?"

"I can think of a reason," he grinned. "A real good one."

"That's blackmail!"

"So sue me."

Reluctantly, Mattie cleared off the table and put the plates in the sink. She wasn't the only deceitful, conniving kid in this house!

That afternoon, Mrs. Almquist collected everyone's composition on the day at the museum. Of course, Mattie had forgotten to write hers. Naturally, Melissa had remembered. Her story was voted best in the class and was entitled, HOW CRUDE THEFT INVADED OUR CULTURAL DAY. Throw-up time!

Mattie could hardly wait till school was out to begin her research. When she arrived at the local library, Mrs. Forsythe was at her usual post, sitting at her desk, smiling and stamping away.

"Hello, dear," she whispered as Mattie entered. "I'm afraid you're too early. It hasn't come in yet."

"What hasn't?"

"The last Agatha Christie book. There's already a waiting list, but I'll be happy to put you down."

"That's not why I'm here, Mrs. Forsythe. I've got a crime of my own to work on now."

"Oh," she chirped excitedly, "that reminds me. I've got something for you." Mrs. Forsythe opened her desk and removed a small gift-wrapped box and handed it to Mattie. "A little thank-you gift."

"For me? What for?"

"Crime detection, of course. Your theory about our

stolen books was correct, Matilda. It was just as you said. Our thief was checking one book out, then returning to the library and slipping the checked card into an unchecked book, thus escaping detection. Once you'd alerted me to that possibility, I wrote down each card number before checking books out. Then I kept my eyes open for suspicious characters. Last week, I apprehended the culprit. I think our crime wave's been broken."

"Terrific. I can cross it off my list of unsolved cases."

"Indeed. But how did you do it?"

"Easy," said Mattie, "but you've got to know the criminal mind, like I do. From the books you said were stolen, I knew the crook was an intelligent guy. So, I put *myself* in his place, then asked myself how *I'd* do it."

"Brilliant," sighed Mrs. Forsythe. "Well go ahead, open your present."

Mattie tore away the wrapping and opened the box. Inside was a bookmark, embroidered with a magnifying glass and cross-stitched with the words: BOOKS MAGNIFY YOUR MIND.

"Gee, thanks. But you shouldn't have bothered, Mrs. Forsythe. This case was a professional courtesy. You always let me take out research books that aren't supposed to leave the library."

"Sshh," she cautioned, glancing around nervously, "that's our *secret*. But tell me, what's this latest case?"

Mattie grew solemn. "The big time. *Art theft*."

"Ohh," said Mrs. Forsythe, obviously impressed. "How fascinating. Did you read that a Degas was stolen yesterday in broad daylight? Wasn't Degas a brilliant artist? His studies of the ballet are inspired. I can understand someone risking his life to own one. Yet there are so many paintings to choose from at a museum. Do you suppose the thief was an afficionado?"

"I don't know his nationality," said Mattie. "Not yet, but I'll find out. I'm going to work up an entire psychological portrait."

"A portrait of an art thief?" Mrs. Forsythe said. "What a clever pun, Matilda. Oh, I so love a well-executed cat-and-mouse game. It makes one's intellectual juices flow. I've never confessed this to anyone, but I find the criminal mind fascinating! In my younger days, I was quite—oh well, never mind. Let's scout out some answers for you, shall we?"

As Mrs. Forsythe hurried toward the art section, her eyes glowed with an intensity Mattie had never noticed before. In all the years she'd been coming to the library, Mattie had had only one impression of the librarian—a kind-hearted, mousey woman, totally devoted to the world of books. She'd always imagined her living alone, a timid widow comforted only by an asthmatic cat. But now, watching Mrs. Forsythe prowl between the aisles, poking through the shelves, she reminded Mattie of a big-game hunter stalking his elusive prey through the treacherous underbrush of the Dewey Decimal System. And seeing that strange twinkle in Mrs. Forsythe's eye as she discussed the theft, Mattie realized she actually knew nothing about the woman. What of her private life? What had she done in her youth? *Did* she live alone? What were her vices, if any? Where did she go on those vacations she never spoke of? Fascinating!

"Here we are," said Mrs. Forsythe, pulling several volumes from the shelves. "These should do nicely." She carried half a dozen books back to the checkout desk. "I'm afraid this is our entire collection. If you need more, the Donnell library has a fine art department. Are you looking for anything specific, Matilda?"

"Everything. What makes an art thief tick? What do forgers have for breakfast? Dad and I are writing an article on art thieves and forgers."

"A collaboration?" she asked, stamping diligently.

"Yeah, but I've got my own case, too. It's confidential."

For a second, Mattie was tempted to confide in Mrs. Forsythe. Would confessing to a librarian make up for not telling a father? No way. Besides, even if Mrs. Forsythe was a pal, she was still a grown-up. And all grown-ups stuck together.

"Oh, mustn't reveal trade secrets," Mrs. Forsythe cautioned. "Everyone has them. Even librarians! I feel it's secrets, not variety, that is the spice of life, don't you agree?"

"That's right," said Mattie. "And mine is a *trade secret*."

"I hope you find what you're looking for," she said, handing Mattie the books. "Oh, I almost forgot," she added, "I'm holding a book for Jonathon." Reaching into her Reserved drawer, she checked out *Turn Your Hobbies into Profits*. "It seems your brother has a new interest. He hasn't borrowed a cookbook in months, just home decorating guides."

"Yeah, he's acting strange," Mattie agreed. "Even for Jono. Every night, he checks the neighbor's trash for old *House Beautiful* magazines. Last Saturday, he spent the whole afternoon in Macy's Sheet Department! Well, thanks for the present, Mrs. Forsythe. See you soon."

As Mattie walked home, she wondered again about Mrs. Forsythe's private life. A dual identity, perhaps? Why not? After all, mild-mannered Clark Kent turned into *Superman*.

Unfortunately, she had no time to dwell on it now. But once her case was solved, she'd definitely investigate!

CHAPTER

4

When Mattie arrived home, she found the door to her and Jonathon's room locked and a scratchy sound coming from inside. She jiggled the knob.

"Don't come in yet," Jonathon shouted. "I'm working."

"Open up, Jono. I've got your book."

Jonathon turned the latch and poked his head out. He had a metal scraper in one hand and paint chips in his hair. "I'm not finished," he explained, blocking the entrance. "It's a surprise."

"What's going on?" asked Mattie, pushing him aside. "What've you been doing?" The bunk had been moved into the center of the room as a divider. A long drapery was strung from the top post to the corner wall. "Why's this here?" she asked, tugging at the curtain. "Setting up a fortune-telling parlor?"

"I've separated my clean, orderly side from your messy, disorganized section," he explained. "I couldn't stand looking at your stuff any longer. Your ratty files and smelly Bunsen burners are driving me nuts. From now on, keep your junk on the other side of that curtain." Jonathon closed the door and continued scraping. "I'm getting this door back down to the wood. These old buildings have fine oak doors. It's a shame they've been painted over."

Mattie watched the paint chips flying. "Have you flipped out?"

"Once it's oiled and waxed, it'll look great." He smiled. "This knob is real brass under the paint. Want to help me polish it?"

"I do not! And how'm I supposed to get to my side, crawl under?"

"Sure, your half's always crawling anyway. Since you won't clean it up—"

"Okay, I didn't make the bunk again. I was in a hurry."

"Look at it!" he said dramatically. "That's no bunk, it's a trough!"

Mattie glanced at their beds. Jonathon's bottom mattress had neatly tucked-in hospital corners. His newly laundered pajamas and robe were rolled and tucked at the foot. But Mattie's looked like a disaster area! A pair of jeans and sweatshirt hung from the bar, two empty soda bottles lay on the rumpled sheet, her comforter hung on the ladder; file folders spilled along the pillows, torn magazines and candy wrappers lay wedged beside the mattress and her deerstalker cap was thrown on the post.

"It's lived in," she said casually.

"By what, a *gorilla*?"

"What do you want from me, Jono, *House Beautiful*?"

"Exactly," he said. "Your half can stay *Mad Magazine*, but not mine."

"This is my *office*: my files, detecting equipment, my microscope and slides, case histories and notebooks. It's all important stuff."

"Well, I need an office, too," he said, resuming his scraping.

"The *kitchen's* your office. I don't complain when you mix up those foul-smelling gravies and sauces. Stick to the stove and quit bugging me."

"The heck I will. I'm branching out. I've been making plans and studying for months. Now I've finally got my first client."

"Are you cooking dinners for Mrs. Hirsch again?"

"This is a *new* career. Being a chef is just the first stage of my master plan."

Mattie pulled open the curtain and dropped the library books on her picnic table. She handed Jonathon his copy of *Turn Your Hobbies into Profits*.

"Does this have anything to do with your big plans?"

"Yeah," he said, dropping his paint scraper. "These how-to books are great. That's where I got the idea to expand my career. And just today, Mrs. Remington gave me my first job."

"What's Melissa's mother got to do with this?"

Jonathon reached in his desk and handed Mattie a slip of paper. "I typed these out last week and slipped them under all the apartment doors."

HIRE THE WEST SIDE'S ANSWER TO
WOMEN'S LIB!

I, The Amazing Jonathon, offers the busy career woman a complete homemaking service!

Ladies: All thumbs in the kitchen?
Do your souffles sink?
Can't boil water?
Tired of your rugs?
Sick of your sofa?
Cats need combing?

DON'T DESPAIR!

Jonathan Cosgrave, creative home engineer, can put your life back in order.
Easy payment plans. Satisfaction guaranteed.

"What's all this about?" asked Mattie.

"Phase Two of my brilliant plan. That's why I was anxious to convince Daddy I could run this house. It's the experience I need. I've already mastered the art of cooking. My next step is to learn interior decorating."

"An interior decorator?" Mattie gulped. "Isn't that sissy stuff?"

"How sexist can you be!" he teased. "Aren't you liberated?"

"Sure I am, but you've already got your hands full cooking for us and running this house. Where'll you find time?"

"That's the great part. Mrs. Remington didn't hire me to cook. She just wants her living room redecorated, and she's given me a month to do it."

Mattie was shocked. "I thought you were happy as a clam, messing around with your stew pots. When did you get this brainstorm?"

"I've been planning it for months," Jono said proudly. "At first, I thought being a chef was a good enough career. Someday, I planned to open my own fancy restaurant. But a guy's gotta be practical. Not many people can afford to eat out these days. So when I saw this Women's Lib craze taking over, I decided to get in on the ground floor. I figured I'd cultivate the talents you females are starting to ignore. In a few more years, you gals will have equal *everything*. Besides catching crooks, you'll be digging ditches, chopping trees and driving garbage trucks.

"But you've all forgotten something! You can't be two places at once. While you're out liberating everything, your houses will be falling apart. There'll be no one to clean, cook or decorate. None of you'll want to hire another female to do such icky work, so that's where I come in. The Amazing Jonathon, Creative Home Engineer! I'll offer a complete home-making service. When these tired ladies come home from a hard day's work in the sewer, I'll have a hot dinner on the stove and clean curtains on the windows. Maybe, after a few years, I'll open franchises and start trainee programs. I'll make a bundle!"

Mattie just stared at him. Up until now, Jonathon's culinary goodies and weird devotion to housework had fit neatly into her scheme of things. He was always available to make the beds and toss the salads. That left her with free time for sleuthing. Now, when she saw that everything had been a part of some great big Master Plan, she felt uneasy. "Sounds goofy to me," she said coolly.

"Well, Mrs. Remington didn't think so," he argued. "She thinks it's *brilliant*. Her living room lacks style, and she's hired me to fix it up. She's given me one hundred dollars to buy things."

"A *hundred dollars*, you're kidding!"

"It's true," said Jonathon. "I've got it here in my desk. I didn't want to take so much money, but Mrs. Remington said it would cost much more if she hired a grown-up. She wants me to buy new scatter pillows, plants, pictures; whatever I like. Mrs. Remington thinks I'm a genius and wants to be my patron."

"That's a lot of money, Jono. It's not safe to leave

it laying around. Only last week, Mr. Horowitz had his boots stolen from outside his door. You need a bodyguard for so much money."

"You want the job?" he asked. "When I go shopping, you can hold the money for me."

"Of course not, I've got my own job. When would I have time?"

"You may have lots of time," he threatened, "if Dad finds out you plan to follow a hot suspect around town."

"Wow, are you turning into a sneaky kid!"

"Runs in the family." He smiled. "How about it?"

"All right, if it doesn't interfere with my surveillance. I've got to start my research, then shadow Mr. Milich tomorrow. What's Mrs. Remington paying for your so-called services?"

"Ten percent," he said proudly. "One hundred dollars expenses, plus ten dollars service charge."

"I'll take half."

"That's *robbery*."

"So sue me. And take down this stupid curtain. It looks ridiculous."

"It's a deal," he said, unhooking the drapes. "They look tacky because they're second hand. Wait'll you see what I do with some *money*!" Whistling, he went back to his scraping.

Later that night as Jonathon was sleeping, his *House Beautiful* fallen to his chest, Mattie lay awake above him thinking over the day's events.

How typical of Jono to think of a better project than hers, and get her to help him. And it was all so easy for him. He didn't have to sneak around evading questions, keeping secrets from Dad. Oh no, Jono slipped blabby posters under doors and got instant results!

But then, things always came easy for Jonathon. It wasn't just because he was younger and got babied more. People always seemed to coo over his talents and admire his creativity. Everyone thought Mattie's interests were crude and unbecoming, but Jonathon's were charming and refreshing. His teachers were thrilled when he brought home-baked cookies to class. Old ladies pinched his cheeks and tousled his hair when he admired their dopey hats. Far from thinking him a sissy, girls found his hobbies "dreamy." And because he liked to polish the brass in the lobby, even Max the doorman, whose vocabulary consisted mainly of grunts, always had a smile for Jono.

Sure, Mattie teased him about mixing up slops in the kitchen, but it wasn't true. Whatever Jonathon did or made turned out right. Except detecting, of course; he was rotten at that.

In spite of everything, though, Mattie'd always felt she had a "calling," while Jonathon merely had a "hobby." But now that she knew his homemaking was only part of broader plans, she had to rethink that, too.

Did she really have a calling, after all? Of course she was dedicated, but was that enough? Could she prove that she was meant to be a detective? This art theft was obviously her great chance. With it, she could graduate from petty larceny into the big time. Everyone would have to take her seriously. Jono's silly Master Plan would pale by comparison!

Once again, Mattie thought of Mr. Milich. Her entire career hinged on exposing him. Was he lying awake too, desperately wondering how to dispose of the stolen Degas? Or was he planning how to spend the money from his ill-gotten gains? Remembering his piercing eyes made her shudder. So much fear in a person's face meant certain guilt. Gosh, if only she could remember where she'd seen that frightened expression before, it might be the clue she needed.

Maybe she hadn't seen Milich in person, before, but she'd definitely seen a photograph. Mattie quickly slipped down from her bunk and began browsing through her FBI folder. No, he wasn't listed anywhere. But maybe her art books had snapshots of suspected forgers and thieves. Excitedly, Mattie grabbed an armful and threw them up into her bed. Then she switched on her night light, pulled a candy bar from under her mattress, and settled down to read.

As soon as she became involved in the book, her uneasy feelings about Jonathon vanished.

CHAPTER

5

Though Mattie lay awake reading for hours, she did not discover the identity of Mr. Milich. But art research was proving to be far more interesting than she'd expected. She still couldn't get excited about the various crocks, canvases and urns people attached so much value to, but the complex personalities of their thieves and forgers was fascinating. The case histories kept her interested far into the night.

Luckily, the next day was Saturday, and she managed to sleep late. At ten o'clock, the smell of pancakes finally lured her into the kitchen.

"Morning, Dad," she said, yawning. "Had breakfast yet?"

"An hour ago," he said. "That's Jonathon's second batch. He tells me he's hired you as his bodyguard."

"That's right. Crazy Mrs. Remington thinks Jono's a genius. I'm not surprised. Melissa and her mother are both mental defectives."

"I wish you children would consult me before getting involved in new projects." He frowned.

"Don't worry, Dad. I'll make sure Jono doesn't buy a lot of junk."

"And get receipts," he cautioned. "Mrs. Remington may want to return your purchases. Why'd she hire you anyway, son?"

Jonathon set down Mattie's breakfast. "She liked my ad and wants to encourage me. Mrs. Remington says I've got great artistic potential. Remember last year's school raffle? She kept the spun sugar swan I made, and never ate it."

"Smart move," snapped Mattie.

" . . . because it was too beautiful to bite," he added. "Besides, Melissa thinks I'm cute."

"How revolting! To change the subject, Dad, I've started on your research, and it's coming along great. I never knew art forgers were such super sneaks."

"Takes one to know one," Jonathon mumbled.

"For instance," she continued, "guess who the first big American art faker was? Paul Revere! In 1770, he was discovered selling "original prints" of a drawing he never did. In 1772, as an engraver, he copied another artist's painting and claimed it was his."

"Guess the history books are wrong," said Jonathon. "Paul must've run through town yelling: 'The cops are coming! The cops are coming!'"

"But here's the weird part," Mattie continued. "Revere was really a silversmith, so while he was counterfeiting pictures, other guys were counterfeiting his silver, stamping his name on everything."

"It's all hard to believe, Mattie," said Mr. Cosgrave.

"That's what's so fascinating about this business," she said. "Art's turned all sorts of good guys into bad guys. Francois Millet's grandson became a millionaire selling pictures painted by his grandfather. Museums bought dozens, but Grandpa didn't paint them. And there are over twelve hundred phoney Corots in this country. He put his name on all his pupils' drawings.

"But the best part was reading how guys knock themselves out trying to make things look authentic. First, they find the proper paper and canvas. To age paper, they treat it with tea. To age canvas, they crack the paint with ultra-violet light. Sometimes to make a clay pot look old, they roll it in ashes, rub it in dirt, then stick it in the ground for years to get it real scrungy looking. Then they sell it to a museum and say some ancient Greek made it."

"You sound like an expert."

"Not yet. Besides it's not quite my line. But there are lots of experts. The New York Police Department has a one-man Art Squad, and there are special scientific labs with lots of fancy equipment. Did you know that pigments suspended in oil can take fifty years to harden completely? But in three minutes, the X-Ray Nondispersive Analyzer can perform analyses that used to take eight hours."

"You sound like a walking encyclopedia," said Mr. Cosgrave, finishing his coffee. "But just what kinds of people steal paintings?"

"First, there's the crazy art collector type. He just steals things because they're beautiful. In 1953, a bronze statue by Rodin was stolen from a London art dealer. A few months later, it was found in the Victoria and Albert Museum with a note under it. The thief said he was an art student who just wanted to live with the statue awhile. Once, in 1911, the Mona Lisa was stolen from the Louvre by an Italian workman. He tucked it under his coat and walked out. They say he had it hanging over his bed at home for two years. The cops finally found it in one of his trunks."

"Amazing," said Mr. Cosgrave. "Can people just walk into museums and steal things?"

"Sure! Besides the Degas taken the other day, just recently a Rembrandt was stolen in Boston and two in Cincinnati. Most museums have lousy security. Once, by accident, some guy got locked inside the Louvre at night and no one was there to let him out. He wandered around for hours. Finally, he found two guards cooking fried eggs on a hot plate."

"That's awful," said Jonathon. "Fried eggs burn

quickly on a hot plate."

"Are most of these found, Mattie?"

"Professional thieves hold most paintings up for ransom. But until they've made contact with a museum or individual, they hide the stuff in weird places. Once, a Rembrandt was discovered stashed in a barn after a hundred-thousand-dollar payoff was taped in an ice machine. A Renoir was hidden in the freezing compartment of an ice cream truck. A Vermeer was found in a graveyard! Another Rembrandt was rescued from under someone's house, covered in bird droppings."

"Art thieves are stupid," said Jonathon. "I wouldn't hide my valuables in such dumb places."

"Where would *you* hide them? Down the hole in your head?"

He smiled smugly. "I've got a super place. I was thinking of putting my one hundred dollars there. Miss Bascomb left a twenty-five pound turkey in the freezer. I plan to stuff it with my money. No crook would ever find it."

"You'd shove a priceless painting into a turkey's fanny?"

"It's better than covering it with *bird doo*!"

"It might work," Mattie agreed, "if the painting were small enough. My book said that's why so many small Rembrandts are stolen. Thieves like small paintings because they can be carried easily and stashed in suitcases."

"Do people steal paintings to carry them around in suitcases, Mattie?"

"Gosh, no, Dad. Most thieves want *cash*. That's why unknown works by famous artists are most valuable to crooks. A painting worth under fifty thousand dollars is much easier to get rid of. Usually, they're not registered and can't be traced. A second-rate painting can be sold to a gallery or a private collector without anyone's knowing it's stolen property."

"Wasn't that stolen Degas worth fifty thousand?" he asked.

"Yeah," said Mattie. "That's probably why the crook picked it. Also, it's small and easy to stash."

Mattie suddenly grew anxious, realizing Anton Milich now had that Degas. Maybe he'd already made contact with a prospective buyer? Her only hope for nabbing him was to find the painting still in his possession. Whether he ransomed it back to the museum or sold it to a private collector, he'd need time to make arrangements. Still, she had to do something soon. Her stakeout of Milich's house had to start immediately. Right now, some unsuspecting Texas oil man, eager to furnish his ranch, might be hitting town. . . .

. . . Sneaky Milich is standing on Times Square, the Degas rolled inside the pocket of his dirty raincoat. Suddenly, he spies an innocent millionaire in leather boots and sequined jacket. "Hey mister," he whispers, "wanna buy a picture—easy payment plans, twenty-five thousand down and ten thousand a week" . . . Or what if Milich was one of those fanatic types who'd snatched the painting for beauty? Then maybe he'd keep it stuffed under his bed the rest of his life! . . .

"You must've sat up all night reading," said Mr. Cosgrave.

"Yeah, Dad, but I enjoyed it. Still, I think it's silly to make such a fuss over pictures and pots."

"Well, after all that reading, you deserve a break. Let's all go biking in Riverside Park."

Mattie hesitated. "No Dad, I'm going to the library. There's lots more books to read: research copies I can't bring home."

"Jonathon?"

"No thanks, Daddy. I've got to oil my door and polish my brass."

"I can't believe it," said Mr. Cosgrave, shaking his head. "Don't kids *play* any more?"

"Hey Mattie," said Jonathon as she left, "while you're at the library, pick me up some more decorating books."

"Sshh," she whispered, "I'm not *really* going to the library. It's my day to stakeout Milich, remember?"

"Because you know more than the entire police department?"

"Exactly, brother dear. The cops have two hundred suspects. They've got to check out everyone in the museum that day. I, on the other hand, already *know* who took the painting. One look into that old

59

man's eyes told me. I've just got to *prove* it."

"Withholding evidence is a crime, sister dear."

"I'm not withholding it, I'm *gathering* it," she argued. "Once I've nabbed this crook, I'll personally take him to the authorities."

"Oh sure, bet all the cops are holding their breath, waiting for Matilda Emmelina Cosgrave, Super Sleuth, to walk into their station house."

Mattie winced. Jono had a way of making precise, professional deductions seem like kooky kid games. Someone should outlaw little brothers!

Mattie returned to her room and checked her bag for essential items: Milich's address, notebook, pencil, subway map, emergency money and several tokens. She combed her hair, slipped into her most comfortable overalls and sleuthing sneakers, then grabbed her deerstalker cap from the bunk post. Looking at herself in the mirror, she smiled approvingly. Her outfit was complete.

Running back to the kitchen, Mattie opened the refrigerator and grabbed a tube of heat-and-serve biscuits.

"What's that for, Sherlock?" asked Jonathon.

"My weapon," she explained. "Milich might be dangerous. I'll need protection. These tubes make a great popping noise if you hit one against a wall. Sounds just like bullets!"

"If it doesn't work, you can always eat it. Want some butter?"

"No thanks. Grease your door with it." Mattie tucked the can into her purse and exited dramatically. "The game's afoot! When next we meet, this case might be solved."

Jonathon sighed. "I'm not holding my breath."

CHAPTER

6

What a perfect day for spying! The sun was bright as Mattie walked along Broadway on her way to the 96th Street Subway Station. Did Hercule Poirot and Miss Marple feel this same twinge of excitement in their work? She couldn't remember.

By checking her map, Mattie knew Mr. Milich's Delancey Street address was somewhere on the Lower East Side. As she passed the subway change booth, she asked directions.

The woman behind the window never ceased shovelling money in and tokens out. "Take the local to 59th Street, change for the D train to 50th, then change for the F train to Delancey & Essex Street."

As Mattie sat in the subway car trying to formulate a plan of action, she found that merely being on a "hot" case made her overly aware of her surroundings. She glanced at her fellow passengers' faces. Poor souls, some of them shuffling off to mundane jobs even on Saturday, punching time clocks and pounding typewriters, while she recaptured a famous national treasure. Yet on the surface, she probably looked as ordinary as they did! What would they all think if they knew her *real* mission? Then again, these subway riders mightn't be what they appeared, either. What did the fat lady in the flattened hat *really* have in that plastic shopping bag? Was the young man slumped in the corner seat with the glazed eyes merely tired or drugged? Did the well-dressed man reading the *Wall Street Journal* neglect to shine his shoes because he was busy, or was he penniless, having lost his last dime in the stock market? On closer examination, even the sweet-faced little boy might turn out to be a brat, a bad seed who'd given his pale-faced mother countless hours of misery.

Mattie became so engrossed in speculation, the forty-five minute ride was over before she knew it. Arriving at Delancey Street, she quickly left the train, leaving the other passengers' lives still mysteries.

Delancey Street was a downtown shopping area in the center of Spanish, Italian, Jewish and Chinese communities. Most of the Jewish stores were closed in observance of Saturday; Sunday had always been the traditional time for bargain hunters on the Lower East Side. But there was now a greater Spanish population, and the street had begun to reflect the change. Sunday was still its busiest sale day, but to Mattie, Saturday was quite crowded enough.

Outdoor stalls covered the avenue as bustling bargain hunters frantically checked the merchandise. Racks of clothing, bins of wigs, hardware, electrical appliances and knickknacks spilled out along the sidewalk. Dozens of shoppers pushed, shoved and haggled, competing for the best buys.

It took Mattie several minutes to make her way down two blocks to number 49, a rundown, graffiti-covered building in the center of a dingy street. She checked the beat-up name plates beside the entrance door. There was a marker for both an A. and P. Milich, with P. Milich crossed out. Apartment 2B.

Strains of Latin music trailed behind her as Mattie made her way up the stairs, past a hallway stacked with garbage bags and trash cans. Wow, the art theft business must be pretty lousy if old Milich had to live in a dump like this!

Cautiously, Mattie glanced down the hallway, making sure no one was around. Leaning her ear against the door of the apartment, she heard the tinny sound of a scratchy foreign record sticking in its grooves. There was a dull but constant shuffling of footsteps.

Mattie peeked through the keyhole. As she was bent over, the doorknob slowly began turning. For a moment, she froze with fear, but quickly dashed up the side stairway.

Mr. Milich opened his door and peeked his head out. Nervously, he glanced down the hall, as if he'd heard something suspicious. Satisfied no one was there, he went back inside and locked the door.

Mattie sat and waited. After several minutes, Mr. Milich came out again, wearing his same soiled raincoat and carrying a parcel—a rolled-up bundle, covered with a plastic bag and tied with string. The Degas! Thank goodness she wasn't too late.

As Milich left the building, Mattie quickly followed after. On the crowded street, she almost lost the old man at first, but as he made his way down the narrow sidewalks of Allen Street, she managed to stay safely several yards behind. Outside a large brick and limestone building wedged between a row of tenements, Milich stopped abruptly. He checked his watch and glanced down to the corner, as if looking for someone. Then clutching his parcel tightly, he climbed the steps of the building and disappeared inside. Mattie rushed to catch up. Pushing by several people standing near the entrance she got inside, just in time to see him scurry through another doorway, to the left of the lobby. Frantically following, Mattie was immediately stopped by a man seated at a desk.

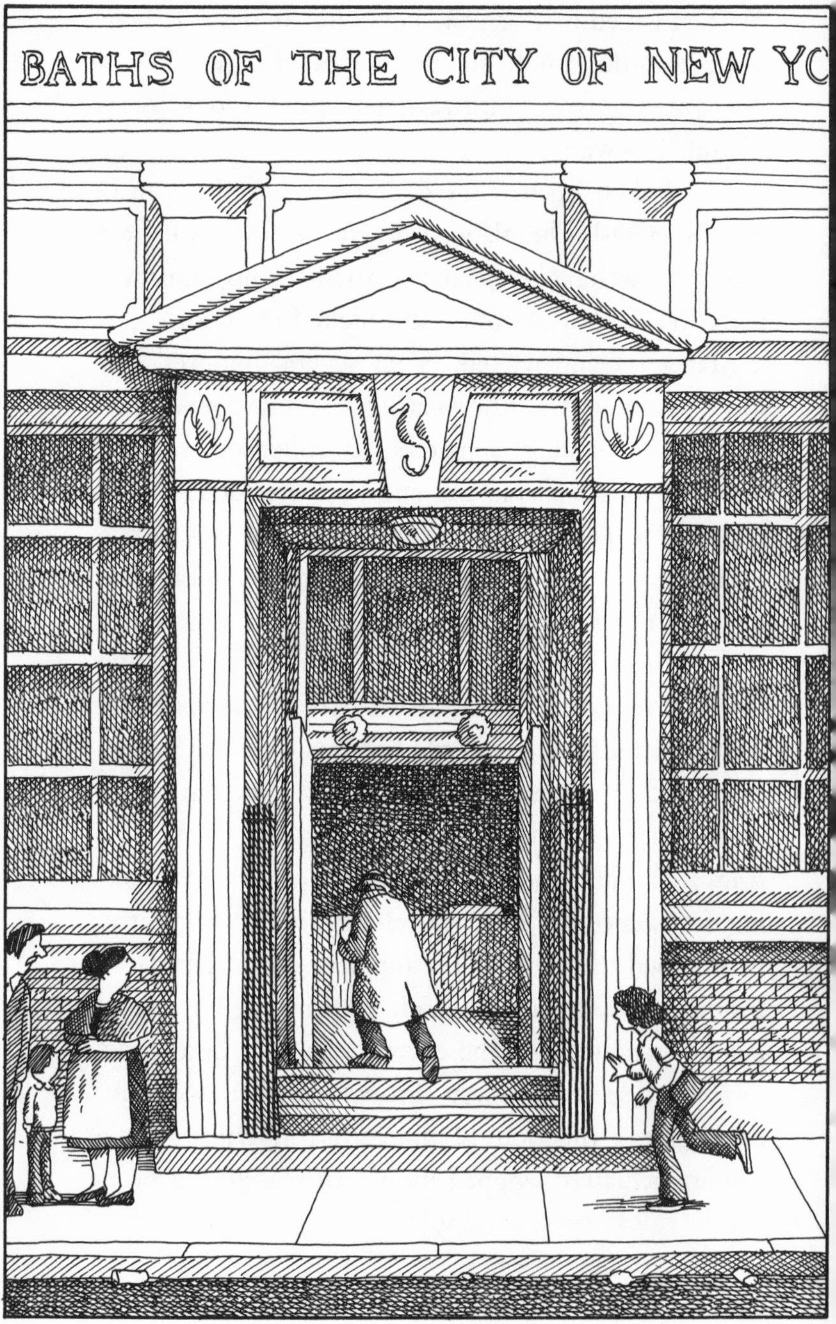
BATHS OF THE CITY OF NEW YO

"Not this way, girlie," he shouted, pointing toward a marble staircase on the opposite side of the lobby, "over there."

"But I'm going in *there*," she insisted.

"This side's for men only."

"Men only? What sexist place is this?"

"Look girlie, Saturday's our busy time. Quit the jokes."

Mattie began wondering what type of peculiar place she'd wandered into. She'd been so intent on following Milich, she hadn't stopped to notice. Then, a small gypsy woman, draped in layers of jewelry and skirts, with three dark-haired children in tow, walked over and took Mattie by the arm. "You new here?" she smiled. "Come, I show you."

"But I want to go in *there*," she repeated.

The three little girls giggled as Mattie kept pointing to the sign saying MEN ONLY.

"Come," smiled the gypsy woman. "I take you."

Reluctantly, Mattie followed her up the marble staircase. She saw what looked like dozens of bathroom booths with women and children passing in and out of the stall doors.

"In there," gestured the woman, pointing Mattie toward an empty booth by the corner wall.

Once inside, Mattie realized it wasn't a bathroom at all, but a shower stall. This must be a public bathhouse! Wow, Milich had outsmarted her. Talk about weird places to hide paintings, this was the *winner*!

If he'd stashed it in an ice cream truck, a graveyard or covered it with bird doo, at least she'd have a chance. But how could she get into a men's shower stall?

Mattie peeked over the shower door, craning her neck to find some way into the men's section. But it was hopeless. An entire floor separated them.

"Look, Mommy," snickered one of the gypsy girls outside the booth. She pointed to Mattie's sneakered feet, sticking from under the door. "That girl has all her clothes on."

The matron glanced toward Mattie's booth as she passed by. "Come on, honey," she said, "get undressed and take your shower. Saturday's our busy time. Folks are waiting."

There were now women waiting patiently on line outside; and suddenly they began staring at Mattie. Well, no sense in arousing suspicion by attracting too much attention. She'd take a fast shower, then slip out discreetly. If she hurried, she could catch Milich before he left the building. She might confront him, make him confess, force him to reveal his hiding place.

Mattie quickly removed her overalls, underwear and sneakers, placing them all on a corner counter. Turning on the hot water, she doused herself. Only then did she realize she had neither soap nor towel. Disgustedly, she shook herself off before redressing. It was hard pulling her clothes on over her sopping-wet body. Her pants stuck to her legs, her hair dripped down her back, and pulling on her socks was *impossible*. She fanned her feet in the air, in a futile effort to dry them. Beneath the shower's door, Mattie suddenly saw the dark-eyed face of the gypsy girl grinning in at her.

Gathering up her things, she unlocked the door just as the matron was passing again. She glanced at Mattie's wet clothing and dribbling curls. "Next time bring a towel, honey. Can't wash right without a towel."

Mattie grinned feebly, placing her bag over her shoulder. Suddenly, she heard a crackling sound. A loud POP! exploded near her ear, and her bag slowly started oozing. A dozen uncooked biscuits began rising and spreading over the side. The heat from the stupid shower must have made the can explode! One by one, they started popping onto the tiled floor. Women and children watched intently as Mattie quickly retrieved the sticky balls, shoving them back into her purse.

The matron stared in disgust. "No food allowed in here. Next time, bring towels."

Mattie's face flushed as she walked sheepishly past the crowded stalls. Starting down the stairs, she could hear the little girl laughing. "Why'd she want to wash in the men's shower, Mommy? Cause she's got big feet? And what's that yucky stuff in her bag?"

All wasn't lost. Coming downstairs, Mattie noticed Mr. Milich exiting from the men's shower room, still carrying his parcel. He was now accompanied by another man, slightly younger and distinguished-looking with graying hair and a well-tailored suit. The accomplice who'd snuck the painting from the museum? The two men were arguing in thick foreign accents.

"No," said Mr. Milich. "I won't do it. It's not right."

"You've got to," the other man insisted. "There's no other way. You agreed."

Could Milich be backing out—feeling guilty about the theft? Or was his accomplice holding out for a higher ransom?

"It's not right, Jacob," Mr. Milich repeated. "Some-one will find out."

"Lower your voice," the other cautioned, glancing around. "At least let's talk about it."

As Mr. Milich clutched his bundle tightly, the man placed an arm around his shoulder, and they both left the building. Mattie hurried down Allen Street in close pursuit. The sun felt warm and good, quickly drying her off. She watched the two men cross Delancey Street, then pause at the corner to begin arguing again. Mr. Milich turned around nervously. Catching Mattie's eye in the distance, he stared at her a moment. Turning around, she busily browsed through a sidewalk bin filled with curly vinyl wigs. She glanced over her shoulder several times. The old man was still *staring*! Even through the crowd of people, Mattie could sense the old man's piercing eyes. Had he recognized her or remembered where they'd met before? If so, he'd certainly know she suspected him of the theft.

"Good buys today," barked the sidewalk merchant. "High class wigs, only a dollar forty-nine. Take a few."

Yes, a disguise was just what she needed. She quickly placed one of the wigs on her head, stuffing her wet hair inside.

"Looks great," said the merchant. "Take two."

"This one's fine," she said, handing him two dollars. She barely had time to grab her change, before her suspects continued down the street. Hurriedly shoving her deerstalker above her wig, Mattie followed.

She trailed them along Delancey Street, passing restaurants, fabric stores, leather goods stores, and just junk shops. Several times, she was afraid she'd lost the men in the crowds of shoppers who pushed along beside her. Yet, she managed to keep track of them.

They passed from one neighborhood to another, and just when Mattie feared her feet might fall off, her suspects finally stopped. They entered a large bookstore where stacks of bargain-priced volumes filled bins and lined the walls. Mr. Milich stopped to check his precious bundle in a locker at the front of the store. Closing the door securely, he placed the

71

key in his pocket. Then the two men began browsing through the bookshelves.

Mattie stationed herself by a corner table and checked the wall clock. Almost four thirty. She'd been walking for hours. Her feet ached, and her stomach rumbled. Glancing inside her purse, she noticed the exploded biscuits. The doughy mess had spread over the bottom of her bag. Much too disgusting to eat, even if she were starving.

Mattie stared at the locker. If only she could snatch that painting! Slowly moving toward the entrance, she discreetly jiggled the door of locker 71. It wouldn't budge. Could she pick it with a bobby pin? No, too many people watching. Anyway, her bobby pins were underneath her wig. She'd have to wait.

Mattie strolled through the store for an hour while the two men browsed through volumes of books, occasionally chatting with one another. Then suddenly, they began arguing again. Several shoppers glanced around in surprise to hear them raising their voices.

Mr. Milich angrily shoved a book back onto the shelf. "It's not enough, Jacob," he shouted. "I've changed my mind."

The other man grabbed him by the shoulder as if attempting to reason with him.

"No." Milich insisted, shaking himself loose. His face flushed with anger, he turned on his heels and stamped out of the store. The other man, suddenly noticing people staring, shoved his hands in his pockets, then quickly followed.

Mattie was stunned. Milich had left without his bundle! What should she do now—follow him or stay with the painting? No sense running all over town. The Degas was safely stashed inside locker 71. She'd stay put until Milich returned for it.

But he didn't! Mattie waited until six o'clock—closing time—but neither man returned. Obviously, something had gone wrong. She recalled what Mr. Milich had said: "It's not enough!" Old Milich must be getting greedy. His accomplice apparently wanted to sell the Degas quickly, but the old man was holding out for a higher ransom.

But as long as Milich held that locker key, there was nothing more Mattie could do. Well, things weren't too bad. She now knew where the Degas was hidden. Once the store closed, even the thief couldn't claim the painting.

As she left the bookstore, Mattie glanced at the hours printed on the window: Monday through Saturday, 9 to 6, Closed Sundays. Thank goodness! She had until Monday morning, more than twenty-four hours, to plan her next move.

CHAPTER

7

In the cool evening air, Mattie shivered through her overalls. Reaching the darkness of the street, she remembered how long she'd been away from home. Her stomach no longer rumbled, it growled. She'd had nothing to eat for eight hours.

Hurrying toward the nearest subway station, she began dreaming of the delectable, tantalizing entrees Jono'd have waiting, knowing Saturday was his chance to lock himself in the kitchen and run wild.

But when Mattie arrived home, both Jonathon and her father were seated in the living room. "Am I late for dinner?" she puffed, throwing her bag on the sofa. "Hope you didn't start without me."

"No, we waited," said Mr. Cosgrave sternly. "We've *been* waiting, more than an hour."

"Guess I'm late. Hope I didn't spoil your super meal, Jono."

"Don't worry," he said, putting down his *House Beautiful*. "It's just hot dogs."

"Hot dogs? That's what I rushed for? No tuna delight or Bavarian beef stew?"

"I was busy and didn't have time. But I'll toast the buns if you like."

Mr. Cosgrave stared at his daughter with a raised eyebrow. "Where've you been all day, Matilda. It's past six-thirty."

Mattie sat down, casually crossing her legs. "Didn't I tell you I was going to the library?"

"That's what you told me," he said coolly. "Yet I can't help wondering if that's actually the case."

"Case?" she asked nervously, throwing a filthy glance toward Jonathon. He shrugged his shoulders, smiling sweetly. "What case?"

"Well, if you've been buried in books all day," her father continued, "why are you wearing that odd contraption on your head?"

Mattie gulped. She'd forgotten to remove her wig. "Oh, this," she laughed, pulling it off to reveal her damp, scraggly hair. "Isn't it cute? I bought it from a street vendor for a dollar forty-nine."

"Quite a bargain," he nodded. "Yet, knowing you, it looks suspiciously like a *disguise*."

"A disguise?" she giggled. "Why would I need a disguise, Dad?"

"Why didn't you get home until six-thirty?" he asked pointedly. "The library closes at five."

While Mattie thought up an excuse, Jonathon quickly jumped into the conversation. "That's my fault, Daddy. I asked Mattie to do some shopping for me. She probably had to search all over town before finding things."

"That's right," she agreed, taking his cue. "Jono ordered weird stuff, but I've got it in my bag."

"May I see?" asked Mr. Cosgrave, taking Mattie's bag from the sofa. He glanced inside. The heat-and-serve biscuits had grown together into one warm, sticky lump. "Very interesting," he said, passing the bag to Jonathon. "Exactly why do you need this?"

With a startled expression, Jonathon peeked inside. "Well," he said haltingly, "it's a special self-rising dough. Great for pizza."

"Indeed?" asked Mr. Cosgrave, calmly clearing his throat. "Well, it's always been my policy never to accuse you of wrong-doing without sufficient evidence."

"Good policy, Dad," said Mattie.

"Let's have our hot dogs now," said Jonathon.

During dinner, there was an uneasy silence. Mattie knew her father suspected something fishy, but he wouldn't do anything until he had proof. From now on, she'd have to be more careful!

When dinner was finished, Mattie went to her room, eager for a long night's rest. Jonathon had spent the day waxing the oak door, polishing the brass knob and generally restoring the room. He'd washed the window, hung fresh cafe curtains, and put down two red scatter rugs he'd found in the closet.

In an attempt to tidy Mattie's corner "pig-pen," he'd tacked a strip of checkered oil cloth around the edge of her picnic table where she kept her important detecting equipment. As a finishing touch, he'd taped up several floral prints cut from magazines.

"Do you like it?" he asked proudly. "It's my *statement*. All decorators make a statement."

"Well," she said wearily, "better get a lawyer before making any more statements. I'm going to bed."

"Be nice to me, Mattie. I got you out of hot water with Dad."

"Yeah, why? What's the deal?"

"There's a super arts and crafts fair tomorrow," he explained. "You're taking me. I've got our day all planned." He handed her a copy of *Wisdom's Child*, the weekly West Side newspaper.

COME TO THE RENAISSANCE OUTDOOR FAIR!

Special Annual Central Park West Event

Join our artists and craftspeople
CRAFTS: Needlepoint—embroidery—

macrame—comforters—quilts
—tie-dyed & batik hangings—
toys—ceramics—stained glass—
hooked rugs

ARTS: Oil paintings—charcoal carica-
tures—original reproductions
(not prints) of famous paintings
done by Adrian, professional
"art faker"—all under $30.00

See Various Craft Demonstrations

COME ONE, COME ALL—FROM NOON TO DUSK

"I'm bringing the whole hundred dollars," said Jonathon excitedly, "so I'll need you as bodyguard."

Mattie climbed into her bed and dumped her stacks of junk to the floor. "Okay," she said.

Jonathon looked puzzled. "No argument?"

"Always glad to help my baby brother."

Jonathon was still looking confused when their father entered to say good night.

"I forgot to ask what you learned at the library today, Matilda."

"Oh, I'm full of facts, Dad. And tomorrow, I'm interviewing Adrian, the famous art forger. He'll make a great psychological portrait for your article. He's exhibiting his paintings at a West Side street fair. I'm taking Jono, too."

"Sounds fine," he said, kissing her good night. As he turned to leave, Mattie could tell something more was on his mind. "Sure you don't want to tell me anything else about today, honey?"

Mattie recalled the promise her father had unknowingly made at breakfast two days earlier. "No, Dad. Everything I'm doing has your official okay."

"Good enough." He smiled. "Have a good sleep."

"What a hunk of baloney," Jonathon whispered as their father left. "Going to that fair was *my* idea. No wonder you were so eager to—"

"Go to sleep," she snapped, closing her eyes.

"Hey, Mattie," Jonathon began as she tried dozing off. "You didn't tell me what happened today. You *always* discuss your cases with me."

Mattie leaned over and glanced down at her brother. When he spoke that way, he seemed like a regular little boy—not a cunning competitor. She was almost tempted to reveal her humiliating experience in the public baths. But she quickly reconsidered. Sooner or later, he'd use it against her!

"Everything went great," she answered. "That painting's safe and sound. Under lock and key, where old Milich can't touch it!"

"Wow, how'd you manage that?"

"Tell you tomorrow." She yawned and turned over.

CHAPTER

8

The next morning, after a long sleep and two helpings of Jonathon's waffles, Mattie was feeling more relaxed and self-assured. While her father mulled over the assortment of Sunday papers, Mattie helped Jonathon clean up the kitchen. As they worked, she filled him in on some of the details of her adventure. She mentioned her trip to the public baths, but carefully omitted the more embarrassing details.

Jonathon's admiration diminished when he discovered the painting was actually stashed in a bookstore locker. "Wow, I thought you had it in a bank vault or something. The whole thing sounds stupid to me. No crook would leave a priceless painting stuffed in a locker."

"You don't know the criminal mind," she argued. "That's a crook's typical M.O. Treating valuables like junk averts suspicion. Old Milich is a clever guy. I bet this isn't the first painting he's snatched. Once I've nabbed him, I'll probably find the stolen Rembrandt, too."

"Well just forget that art thief," he said. "If you want half my profits, you'd better think about bodyguarding."

"Don't worry," said Mattie, drying the last dish. "I've got a super place for your cash. I'm sticking it under my innersoles. If I get mugged, they'll have to steal my sneakers."

"That'll keep'm off the scent," said Jonathon. "A sniff in your sneakers would knock a guy unconscious."

When the housework was done, the two got dressed. Jonathon gave Mattie his twenty five-dollar bills, which she slipped into her sneakers.

"We're off to the fair, Dad," said Mattie, grabbing her pad and pencil. "See you at dinner."

Mr. Cosgrave peeked over his newspaper. "What're we having tonight, son? Pizza?"

Jonathon stared blankly. "Yeah, sure." On the way out, he poked Mattie in the ribs. "I don't know how to make pizza," he whined.

"Forget it. We'll pick one up on Broadway."

"Not with *my* money."

"Okay," she groaned, shoving him into the elevator. "My treat."

Golden leaves were scattered along the street as the two of them strolled toward Central Park West. A police department sawhorse blocked off traffic down the side street, and a large red banner hung above the buildings announcing THE RENAISSANCE FAIR. Crowds of people lined the sidewalk, wandering from booth to booth.

To Mattie, it was as if they'd turned a corner and stepped into another time. Two strolling troubadors, wearing striped tights and jerkins, strummed medieval melodies on mandolins. A woman dressed in colonial costume was seated beside a large quilting frame, putting the finishing touches on a log cabin quilt. An old man busily made corn husk dolls, grabbing dried stalks from a box by his feet. Three young girls knotted rubber bands around tee-shirts, showing the crowd the steps in tie-dying. Dozens of booths and exhibits crowded every inch of sidewalk, and concessions sold homemade baked goods, fresh cider and fruit, as well as handcrafts.

"This is terrific," said Jonathon, stopping by a table lined with patchwork pillows. He selected one of satin squares in various shades of blue. "Just the thing for Mrs. Remington's sofa. Only seven fifty."

The old woman seated at the table smiled proudly. "I've been making them for years. There's a story behind every patch. That green one. . . ."

"We don't have time to hear it," whispered Mattie, poking Jonathon. Slipping two bills from her sneaker, she handed them to the old woman who put the pillow in a bag.

"Hold it for me?" asked Jonathon. "I'll be back later."

They continued down the street, and within an hour, Jonathon had bought a hanging planter made of blue-glazed ceramic, four peacock feathers, a carved wooden sculpture of a bird, a blue hooked rug and a tie-dyed wall hanging. He'd spent a grand total of fifty-six dollars for the items, all of which he considered fantastic bargains. At each booth, Mattie paid, and Jonathon asked to have his purchases held.

"Sure hope Mrs. Remington wants this stuff," Mattie grunted. "I wouldn't give a nickel for it." She glanced down the street, "Wonder where that art faker, Adrian, is set up."

"Don't rush me, Mattie. Decorators need time to make decisions."

Three purchases and a half hour later, after seeing a stained-glass demonstration, watching a charcoal portrait done, plus discovering how to macrame, they finally reached Mattie's point of interest.

A large booth with a banner reading, ADRIAN, FAMOUS ART FAKER, had drawn a sizeable crowd. Propped along the side of the building were stacks of canvases, all "original reproductions" of famous artists: Renoir, Matisse, Degas, Cezanne. Though many were of the same painting, each was slightly different. In one pastel, a Degas ballet dancer had a pink costume, while in a similar one, the dancer wore white. In one version of Picasso's *Lovers*, the man wore orange as in the original: in another, green.

"These are really good," said Jonathon, poking through the canvases.

Standing beside the canvases was a tall, slender man. He had long black hair and a well-cropped beard. His black eyes sparkled. Elegantly dressed in a silk ascot and velvet jacket, he tapped his silver walking stick against the pavement. "You're a true art connoisseur, young man," he said, smiling at Jonathon.

"Are you Adrian?" asked Mattie, reminded of pictures she'd seen of Salvadore Dali, the way-out looking painter.

"At your service, Mademoiselle. Feel free to browse. At these prices, there's something for everyone."

"Hey, are you really a *forger*?" asked Jonathon. "That's against the law."

Adrian laughed self-assuredly, taping his walking stick as punctuation. "*Au contraire*. I'm a *faker*, not a forger. Those who buy my works know they're not genuine. If you'll notice, they all bear my own signature."

"Gee, you painted every one?" asked Mattie, gazing at the array of famous artists represented.

"Not just one, but many of every one," he added.

"Adrian," called a woman. "Have you any Mary Cassat? I simply go mad over her little girls."

"Yes indeed. If you'll excuse me, children?"

"Look at this," said Jonathon, browsing through a pile of Degas canvases. "Isn't this a copy of the painting that was stolen?"

Mattie glanced at the picture. A bowl of pink and beige seashells lay in the background. In the center of a cloth-covered table were a collection of cucumbers, lemons and limes. As with all Adrian's paintings, each version was signed by him, but had slight variations.

"It's just like the photo in the paper," said Mattie, suddenly realizing she'd never actually *seen* the picture. "So that's what's hidden in locker 71!" She stared at it in disappointment. "It doesn't look like much to me."

"Oh, I like it," said Jonathon, selecting one from the pile. "This one's the prettiest. Won't it look great on Mrs. Remington's wall?"

"That one's got a sold sign, Jono," she said, noticing the red sticker in the corner. "Pick another."

"But this one's the best," he insisted. "These limes are the exact shade of Mrs. Remington's drapes. Just my luck, the painting I want has a sold sticker."

Adrian returned to see Jonathon examining the picture. "That one's spoken for," he said, placing it aside. "Are you a Degas fancier, young man? Well, for thirty dollars, you can also be a Degas owner."

"Yeah, but that's the nicest one," he pouted. "Why'd you switch the colors in the others?"

"Aha," Adrian sighed, "all artists thrive on variety —the spice of life, you know. Even when copying, one must make a personal statement."

"Jono knows all about statements," said Mattie. "He's an interior decorator."

"Ah, a *professional*." He smiled approvingly. "In that case, you deserve a professional discount." He pulled another version of the Degas from the pile, handing it to Jonathon. "You may have this one for half price, fifteen dollars."

"Gee, that's nice of you," said Mattie. "Could you do *me* a favor, too? My dad and I are doing an article for his newspaper, profiling art forgers. Can you tell me what you guys are really like?"

"Faker, my dear," he corrected. "*Faker*."

"Yeah, okay. Maybe you could fill me in on your art training?"

"Gladly," said Adrian, obviously flattered by the attention. "As a young man, I studied at the Sorbonne in Paris. I was a gifted student. . . ."

As Mattie feverishly began taking notes, Jonathon continued staring at his fifteen-dollar Degas. It just wasn't as nice. The green was definitely not Mrs. Remington's drapes. He glanced back at the painting with the sold sticker. *That* was her drapes exactly!

". . . .Unfortunately," Adrian continued, "Americans are more interested in *dead* artists, than living ones. So several years ago, I decided to channel my talents in another direction. It had been difficult selling my own work, but I have found faking other peoples' work to be quite lucrative. Alas, these paintings may not have my style, but at least they have my signature. Who knows, perhaps someday a fake Adrian may be more valuable than a real Picasso. Until then, I make do."

"Very interesting," said Mattie, writing everything down. "So there's big money in fakery?"

Adrian shrugged his shoulders. "For one with my great talent, yes. I keep prices low and rely on volume. It's a living! Now tell me, young lady, in what paper will this appear? Publicity always helps, if one's name's spelled correctly."

While Mattie told Adrian her father's name and the paper he worked for, Jonathon tucked his Degas underneath his arm.

"Give him the money, Mattie," he prodded impatiently, "before he changes his mind about the discount."

Mattie dug into her sneaker and pulled out three bills, handing them to Adrian. "Dad's feature is coming out next month in the Sunday supplement."

"I'll be looking for it." He smiled.

"Jono," coaxed Mattie, "thank the nice man for your bargain."

"Sure," he said, holding tight to his painting.

"Thanks a lot. C'mon, Mattie, let's go."

"What's your rush?" she asked, putting away her notebook.

"*C'mon*," he insisted, tugging at her. "Let's see the rest of the fair."

By five o'clock, Jonathon had bought two more handmade pillows, a small stone carving and still had nine dollars left. They strolled back down the street, picking up each purchase from the booths as they went. Jonathon glowed with satisfaction as he carried home his two shopping bags full of treasures.

Stopping on Broadway, Mattie picked up a pizza as promised. In a good mood after getting her exclusive interview, she hardly minded spending the money.

Mr. Cosgrave was in the shower when the two of them went into the apartment, so Jonathon was able to sneak his pizza into the kitchen without any trouble.

"Hope Dad isn't suspicious," he said, throwing the box in the trash. He opened a can of anchovies, got some cheese, spread them on top of the pizza, then he shoved it into the oven. "Now I can say I made it."

"Let's take this stuff up to Mrs. Remington," said Mattie, unpacking his bags. "I want to see her face when she discovers what you bought."

"Oh no," said Jonathon, replacing the purchases and carrying the bags to their room.

"Why not?" asked Mattie.

Jonathon spread the things along his bunk bed and propped the painting on the end table. "I want to *look* at them all." He sighed. "Aren't they beautiful? I like the painting best."

Mattie stared at the small oil painting with Adrian's signature prominently displayed in black letters in the upper corner. "It still doesn't look like much," she confessed. "But I think it's just as good as stuff in museums. Why people consider some valuable and others junk is a mystery to me."

"That's because you've got a detective's soul," said Jonathon scornfully. "Only a truly sensitive person with an artistic eye can detect the subtle difference. This painting's pretty, but nothing like an original." With a self-satisfied air, Jonathon walked toward his desk. "I think I'll draw up a plan of Mrs. Remington's living room before deciding where things go." Opening the drawer, he knocked a small file folder to the floor. Bits of paper came spilling out.

"What're these?" asked Mattie, collecting them up.

"They're mine," said Jonathon nervously, trying to grab them back. "They fell from my file."

Mattie clutched the papers behind her back. "*Your* files?"

"You're not the only one with files. Give them here."

"Not so fast, let me see."

Mattie began reading the brief messages on several slips of paper:

This ham was inspected by No. 63. It has been packed by the Marston Packing Company under exacting standards. Thank you for buying this ham.

Under the message, was a notation in Jonathon's handwriting:

Dear No. 63: Your ham was salty with too much gristle.

Mattie read another:

Every precaution has been taken to make this jam the best money can buy. Our jams are carefully inspected and we sincerely hope it meets your approval. I personally checked this jam—Evelyn Dofflemyer.

This one said:

Dear Evelyn: Not enough strawberries.

Still another read:

We at Ballard Ltd. manufacture sweets of the highest quality. If you have any complaints, please return the remainder of your uneaten sweet and we will happily refund your money.

Dear Ballard Ltd: Broke my filling on it. The soft centers were hard!

And another:

This mattress cover has been manufactured from 100% virgin vinyl. It will give you a life time of wear.

Here, Jonathon wrote:

It ripped! And what the heck's virgin vinyl?

There were dozens of slips of paper with Jonathon's sappy replies, but he pulled them from Mattie's hands before she could read them all.

"What is this junk? Diaries of a mad housewife?"

"It's my pen pal file," he answered sheepishly. "Lots of companies pack notes with their products, and I always answer them. Sometimes, they send me samples and coupons. That jam on your waffles this morning was compliments of Evelyn Dofflemyer. She sent me a coupon for a free jar."

"So what's the big secret? Why act like a criminal?"

"That's all you think of," he snapped. "Not just criminals keep secrets, you know. Regular people have them, too! I keep my files hidden because I knew you'd laugh at them. You always laugh."

Mattie watched as Jonathon picked up the remainder of his spilled folders and replaced them in his desk. Was he right, she wondered. Did everyone have some secret, a vulnerable section of life locked away from the world? Even creepy kid brothers?

"Time to take the pizza from the oven," said Jonathon. "But don't tell Dad a word about buying it. That's *our* secret."

After dinner, Jonathon proudly displayed all his purchases for his father.

"Very tasteful," smiled Mr. Cosgrave. "But I hope your client's prepared for all this art."

"I like the painting best," said Jonathon. "These limes are a perfect compliment to Mrs. Remington's drapes. I'm going to hang it right over the sofa, where. . . ."

Jonathon rattled on as Mattie picked the anchovies off her pizza. They'd had such a busy day at the fair, for a few hours she'd forgotten about the old man and the stolen Degas. But now, it all came rushing back, and with it, a twinge of guilt. She'd have to play hooky from school tomorrow. There was no other way to be in that bookstore at nine o'clock. She must be there to nab the old man when he took the painting from the locker.

It was too bad she had to deceive her father again, but she had no alternative. She consoled herself with the thought that maybe he, too, had some secret. Anyway, once the Degas was recovered, he'd be too proud of her to be angry.

Besides, she wouldn't be in any real danger. Mr. Milich was a thief, but at least he wasn't dangerous or *violent*. Or was he? Remembering the terrified look in the old man's eyes, Mattie began to wonder!

CHAPTER

9

The next morning, Mattie got up early to help Jonathon clean the house. She hoped being charitable and sisterly as the day began would make up for the sneakiness she planned. Of course, she didn't tell Jono about her hooky plans. She didn't actually think he'd snitch, but it never hurt to be cautious.

Jonathon was still so caught up in his precious purchases, he spent most of his time admiring them. As Mattie dusted and washed the dishes, he babbled on about their various shades of blue and green. Mattie even had to make her own lunch.

And lucky she did. By eight thirty, Jono'd gotten so far behind in the morning chores, she had a perfect excuse to leave for school without him.

"I've gotta run," she shouted, throwing her sandwich into a bag. "See you later."

Instead of turning down West End Avenue toward school, Mattie continued to the Broadway subway station. The rush hour crowds jamming into the cars took no notice of her. Yet Mattie felt every strap hanger stared at her accusingly, as if she were wearing a huge sandwich board, announcing:

> I'M PLAYING HOOKY TODAY! MY FATHER, A KIND, CONSIDERATE MAN, WOULD DIE IF HE KNEW!

At the station nearest the bookstore, Mattie was washed along in the sea of bodies that floated out the doors. Walking quickly toward the bookstore, she arrived moments after it opened. She casually came in with several other early morning shoppers. Passing the entrance, she checked locker 71. It was still securely locked. Strolling to the back of the store, she began browsing through the mystery novels, at the same time keeping a watchful eye on the door.

It was nearly ten o'clock when Mr. Milich arrived. Mattie could hear her pulse thump faster as she spied him coming in. Wearing the same disheveled outfit, he slipped the locker key from the pocket of his dirty raincoat.

Cautiously, Mattie moved toward the entrance, making sure the old man didn't notice her. She was standing directly behind him as he pulled the fifty-thousand-dollar bundle from its hiding place and tucked it under his arm.

Mattie's heart beat faster as she froze in a moment of indecision. What now? Should she snatch the painting and run toward the nearest police station, or confront the old man, demanding a full confession?

Mr. Milich turned in startled surprise to see her standing behind him. His frightened gray eyes were filled with guilt and apprehension. He stared at her searchingly, with a look of sudden pained recognition.

"You," he said in a shaky whisper. "You—again?"

Reaching out a trembling hand to touch hers, Mattie noticed his expression wasn't one of guilt so much as sadness.

"Vesna?" he whispered, his eyes staring as if in a dream. "No, it can't be so." He grabbed Mattie's hands, pulling her toward him. "Vesna?"

Mattie's throat turned to a dry lump. Stepping backward, she pulled her hands away, but couldn't avert the old man's glazed eyes.

"Is true?" he continued. "I have seen you before?"

"Yeah," she said, choking out the words. "At the museum, the day the painting was stolen."

"Ah yes," he nodded, strangely relieved. "Is true. Sometimes, an old man's memory plays tricks. Ghosts from the past come back to haunt."

Mattie had no idea what he meant. She wanted desperately to grab his bundle and run. But his search-

ing, pleading expression made her stop.

"They'll find you," she said threateningly.

"Is no matter now," he said with a shrug. Reaching over, he grabbed her hand again. "Who are you, child?" he demanded. "Come. We must talk."

"Don't come near me," said Mattie, her voice quivering.

She'd been a fool! She should've called the police before entering the bookstore. By now, a squad car could be circling the block, their lights flashing and bull-horns blaring. . . . MILICH, DROP THE PAINTING AND COME OUT WITH YOUR HANDS UP. LEAVE THAT BRAVE LITTLE GIRL ALONE! . . .

Yet all wasn't lost. If only she could convince this old guy the cops were waiting outside, she'd be safe.

"I've been followed," she said grimly. "So don't try anything funny."

"Yes," he nodded sadly. "They always follow. Ghosts from the past never rest easy."

What was he saying? Milich kept babbling about ghosts! Gosh, was he a *murderer* as well as a thief?

"Come," he repeated, clamping his arm on her shoulder. "We must talk!"

Mattie did some split-second thinking, desperately puzzling out her next move. If Milich was more than an ordinary art thief—perhaps a crazed weirdo who'd killed someone—she'd better humor him. Killers carried knives and guns. She didn't even have her biscuit can! But if she could lure him into a restaurant—

someplace with a telephone—she could call the police.

"Sure," she said, straining to sound casual. "Let's talk. I'm awfully thirsty. Can we get a soda?"

The old man nodded, and with his hand still gripping her shoulder, led her through the door of the bookshop. Mattie glanced back, frantically hoping someone would notice her "kidnapping." But the customers paid no attention. She felt her legs turn to jelly as they walked along the avenue, stopping at a corner coffee shop.

Once inside, Mr. Milich placed his package in the booth beside him. Nervously, Mattie glanced around. There was a phone booth by the wall. As the waitress came by to take their order, Mattie gave her a knowing wink, nodding in the direction of the telephone.

"What'll it be?" asked the waitress, without glancing up from her pad.

"A cherry Coke," said Mattie, desperately winking and gesturing.

"Please, a cup of tea?" asked the old man.

"Tea and Coke," she nodded, turning away, leaving Mattie alone with her abductor. Obviously, she'd have to try a different approach.

"I think I'll call my father," said Mattie, a thin note of panic rising inside her. "He planned to meet me at the bookstore. I'd better tell him I've left, because when he gets nervous he does crazy things." (Why had she used the word "crazy"? Weirdos always *hated* hearing that word!)

Mr. Milich stared at her with an odd, unsettled glance. "Is not good for children to disobey. Terrible things can happen."

Ignoring the threat, Mattie continued. "Once, when I came home late, my dad called out the *police department*." Nervously, she fumbled through her purse for a dime. "I'll let him know I'm safe."

"Is good," said the old man. "Children must take care. Vesna, she would not listen. Now, is too late."

As Mattie rose from the table, Mr. Milich's eyes filled with tears. "Is too late," he stammered. Feeling through his raincoat for a handkerchief, he found none. "Forgive an old man's tears," he continued, "but seeing you brings back such memories."

Mr. Milich took his bundle from the seat and placed it on the table. Ripping open the covering, he fumbled through a wad of rolled-up towels until he found a clean white handkerchief. Blowing his nose loudly, he shoved the handkerchief into his pocket.

Mattie stared down at the bundle—which she'd been following for two days—unable to believe her eyes. Laundry! The stolen Degas was actually an old man's shirts and towels. Her head buzzed with confusion.

"The painting!" she gasped. "Where is the *painting*?"

"Ah yes," said Mr. Milich. "The museum is where we met. I remember staring at you. You looked so much like my Vesna. That same sparkle in your eyes.

For a moment, all the memories returned, all the pain."

The waitress arrived and set down their order of tea and Coke. Mr. Milich took a sip from his cup. "You must call your father, yes?"

"That can wait," said Mattie, eager to solve this new puzzle. "If you didn't take . . . I mean, why'd you act so sneaky? That day in the museum, you were afraid of being searched. You tried to leave before the police came. Why?"

The old man smiled wryly. "How can one so young, so innocent, understand? In this country, the police are to protect you, yes? But in my country, this was not always so. In Yugoslavia during the war, the police were something to fear."

"Then you *are* a crook?"

"No, my child," the old man sighed. "A Jew. A word I can speak now, but in the time of the Nazis, one which must only be whispered. People like me, without the proper papers were often hunted down like animals. The lucky ones lived like fugitives, sheltered in attics and storerooms, protected by loyal friends, or they did not live at all. Years pass, but those days of horror can't be forgotten. That day in the museum when I saw you, my nightmare came back to haunt. You looked so much like my Vesna, the daughter who died during the war."

Mattie felt too awkward to answer. All her clever deductions had led to this—an old man with memories. "I—I don't understand," she mumbled.

"It was also in a museum," he explained. "Already, many Jews had gone underground. Belgrade had been bombed twice. My Vesna was twelve. A quiet child, always loving beautiful things. She begged I take her to the museum that day. I was frightened. Public places were never safe for Jews. But she insisted. Just before the bombs hit, she strayed in the crowd. Within minutes, the side of the building was destroyed. Later, they found her body in the rubble."

Mattie was stunned by the old man's story. "Oh, that's awful," she whispered. "Was she your only child?"

"Yes," he murmured. "When it was over, I tried to get my wife to leave the country—escape if we could—forget the past. But she could not part with her home and loved ones. You see, she wasn't Jewish. She came from a wealthy family and had many relatives she couldn't bear to leave. I only had one older brother, living in New York. So we stayed—endured the war. My Elena was certain we'd be safe. But in that last year, the Nazis . . ." Mr. Milich paused, his voice quivering on the brink of tears. Finally, he sipped his tea and resumed his story. "But all that is past and best forgotten. Last year, when my dear Elena died, my brother vouched for me, and I came to this country on a visa. Then last month, my brother died also. So now, I am alone. My visa has expired, and I must go back. A neighbor in my building—always he tries to convince me to stay—move in with him so no one will find out. Then no one will know I'm living here illegally. But is not enough, just to live. One must have peace of mind."

"Isn't there anything you can do?" asked Mattie.

"Perhaps," sighed Mr. Milich. "But I'm a tired old man who has seen much. I can run and hide no longer. What is to be, must be. Always, I'm afraid my papers will be checked, I'll be deported. Such is not the way to live."

"So that's what scared you that day in the museum when the police searched everyone?"

"That's right. Also, I remembered those days of the Nazi occupation. I heard someone mention a *bomb*. Then, I saw you and remembered my Vesna. You look so much like her, child. It was as if the nightmare was happening again. The beauty in my world being destroyed—again."

Mattie felt a hard lump growing in her stomach. Once she'd heard the old man's story, it was impossible to imagine she'd ever suspected him of being a criminal.

"I'm sorry," she whispered. "Sorry about everything. That day in the museum, I thought *you* stole the painting. That's why I've been spying on you. I followed you to the public baths and saw you hide that bundle in the locker. I thought it was the Degas."

"Is all right," said Mr. Milich, attempting a smile. "I was a suspicious character, yes? You discovered a thing of beauty had been stolen and were eager to find it? During the war in my country, much art was lost. Soldiers would come. There'd be much looting and burning. Many treasures were lost. Is good you wanted to help."

"Gosh, no," she confessed. "I don't like the painting. I just wanted to catch the thief. When I first saw you, I was certain you'd done it. This was my chance to catch a big-time crook."

"Crook?" asked Mr. Milich, puzzled. "What is this?"

"A criminal," Mattie explained. "Oh, I know lots about their minds because I'm a detective. I try to get inside people's heads and figure why they do things. You know, psychology? And faces tell lots about a person. But research is important, too. And instincts, of course. A good detective needs them *all*."

Mr. Milich looked confused. "Detective? Is such an ambition for a young girl? Ah, but in this country, there is freedom to do *everything*. Is good."

"Yeah well," she added glumly, "so far all I've done is make mistakes. You were my one big lead. I was certain you were the thief and your friend was an accomplice. Now, I find out all you were hiding was *laundry*."

I live in what you call a cold-water flat," he explained. "Each day, I bring towels and wash at the public baths. My friend Jacob, always he comes to my room—follows me—talks to me of staying in this country, breaking your laws. Each day, I try to avoid this. He made me so angry, I forgot my bundle in the bookstore. I remembered only this morning when the locker key fell from my raincoat."

"All your sneaking around makes perfect sense when you explain it," Mattie sighed.

"But now you have lost your suspect, yes? Your time has been wasted on a foolish old man who thinks he sees ghosts."

"No," said Mattie, "you're a *nice* old man. But you're not the thief."

"And is so important you catch him?"

"This was my first major crime," she explained. "And it happened right under my nose. But it didn't really. Now I know the thief must've left the museum before my class arrived. That means I'll never find him. I'm a total failure."

"Never to think that," said Mr. Milich sympathetically. "One must never give up. Always, we must look for the good in everything." Taking Mattie's hand, he smiled. "You say you have found nothing. Yet *I* have found a great deal. For a few moments, I have found my Vesna again."

CHAPTER

10

When Mattie said good-bye to Mr. Milich, her head was in a daze. She began wandering aimlessly, seeing no point in returning to school nor wanting to go home.

Strolling along, she realized how drastically her life had changed. Shortly before, she had seemed moments away from fame and success. Now, there was no possibility of *ever* finding the art thief. Some detective! She might just as well call up everyone in the New York phone directory, asking them if they'd stolen a Degas.

Mattie felt as if any moment the street might split open, swallowing her up beneath it. There was nothing left in life to rely on. Her female instincts *stunk*!

Nearing Washington Square, Mattie wandered through the tiny park and sat down on a corner bench. She opened her lunch bag and took a bite of her tuna fish sandwich. But she couldn't eat. Her brain kept swimming with muddled images—poor old men and faithful fathers—wars and bombs and stolen paintings—Vesna's ghost and Degas' ghost—exploding biscuit cans and broken dreams. Her mind was a mess!

Mattie's stomach rolled over and her head pounded. Taking her lunch bag, she dumped it in the trash can, then leaned in after it. She was definitely going to be sick!

Mattie spent the rest of the afternoon wandering around, never quite certain where she was. At four o'clock, she found herself staring at her greenish reflection in a Macy's display window and decided to go home. Half an hour later, weary and disgusted, she pushed open the apartment door, dragged herself into the bedroom and flopped on her bunk. Rest and quiet was all she wanted.

Jonathon was seated on his bunk, picking up the pieces of a game. "Hey," he said, "did ya see Richie Hirsch and Melissa Remington on your way up in the elevator? They just left and had that same hang-dog expression." Continuing to chuckle, he shuffled his paper money and replaced it in the box. "There's been so much talk about art around here, I decided to dig out my MASTERPIECE game," he explained. "Wow, did I beat the pants off them! Of course, I was the banker. I started with one million five hundred thousand dollars and wound up with four million. Richie got all the forgeries, and all Melissa's paintings had to be sold for a loss at private auctions. Dealing with art's not hard when you know what you're doing," he said smugly, returning the game to the shelf. "Of course, you've gotta be on your toes and not get fooled by forgeries."

Mattie lay in silence, trying hard to ignore Jono's bragging.

"I've been thinking," he continued, "there's big money in this art stuff. Businesses and hotels spend fortunes hiring people to decorate their offices and lobbies with original paintings. It might be a mistake to limit myself to creative engineering for ladies. Yeah, I could turn Phase Two of my career into something *bigger*. With my talents, instead of just fixing up apartments, I could manage a whole hotel!"

"Please shut up, Jono," said Mattie numbly, her head beginning to pound.

"Sure," he said, obviously thrilled by his newest idea. "I could be a chief chef, interior decorator, *and* art consultant. After all, if *you* can learn about art, *anyone* can. With my creative abilities, there's no limit to what—"

"Shut up, Jono," Mattie repeated, trying to control her anger, "*I'm warning you*." While she wallowed in failure, she had no intention of listening to his Master Plan to control the world!

"Of course, I'd begin small," he added. "Just in New York. But in a few years, I could turn it into an international business."

"That's enough!" she shouted, throwing a pillow his way.

"What's with you?" he asked in surprise. "Oh, don't worry, when I'm rich and famous, I won't forget you, Mattie. I'll give you a job in one of my hotels as a house detective."

That was the last straw! Unable to control herself a moment longer, Mattie climbed down from her bunk and stared at him in purple rage. "Why stop there, Mr. Big-Man!" she screeched. "Since you're so brilliantly talented, you can be the house detective, too!"

Seized with anger, Mattie ran over to her detecting table, knocking her books and files to the ground. "Here," she smoldered, "take these for a start." Frantically ripping up her papers, she scattered them in the air. "And these, too. Take them all."

Jonathon stared hang-mouthed, speechless at last. He watched in disbelief as Mattie ripped the oil cloth from under her table and hurled it in his direction. Then she kicked her box of test tubes toward the corner and stomped on her deerstalker cap. "Take *everything*!" she shouted. "I don't want it anymore."

Still in a frenzy, Mattie went about her side of the

room, systematically overturning every box, jar and folder. "Here, how about some wallpaper?" she shrieked, ripping her numerology chart from the wall and hurling it at him. "And here's something to stuff your home-baked cookies in," she added, kicking at her fingerprint specimen cannisters. "These might come in handy to detect art forgeries," she sneered, dumping out her collection of magnifying glasses and scrunching them into a pitiful pile of broken glass. Still in a state, she trampled on her code decipher ring. Not one item of detecting equipment escaped her wrath.

"Who's gonna clean up this mess?" Jonathon demanded.

"Who do you think?" she screeched. "After all, you're The Amazing Jonathon!" Gazing around at the mess she'd created, Mattie noticed one last item still intact. In final protest, she picked up her inkwell. In a last gesture, she held it threateningly above her head. "Here," she shouted, "use this to write me your bill. And don't forget your easy payment plans!"

As Jonathon saw the bottle heading his way, he ducked, narrowly avoiding being hit. The inkwell sailed across the room, smashing into Mrs. Remington's painting, which was propped against the end table.

"Now you've done it, you rat," he whined. "That better be disappearing ink or you're in big trouble!"

Jonathon ran over to the painting. Dark blue ink

dripped down one side, covering all the lovely pink and beige seashells. In a futile attempt to salvage it, he quickly snatched Mattie's pillow from the floor, pulling off the cover. But blotting the surface only made it worse, causing the horrible blue blob to spread even further. "Gee, why'd you do it?" he asked in hurt confusion.

Mattie stood motionless a moment, stunned by what she had done. She glanced over at Jonathon. He was cradling the painting on his lap, still dabbing the splotch with her pillowcase. "It was so pretty," he whimpered, trying to hold back tears. "Of all the things I bought, it was the nicest."

"It's your own fault," she shouted hotly. "I told you to shut up, but you wouldn't listen."

"My fault?" he cried. "You never listen to me, either! Only what *you* do is important. *My* stuff's always silly and sissy and doesn't count. But I've got rights and feelings, too!"

As waves of guilt and anger mixed inside Mattie, she felt sick and weak in the knees. "Oh, go away," she shouted, throwing herself onto her bunk. "Why can't you leave me alone!"

CHAPTER

11

Jonathon did not utter another word. In stony silence, he left the room, retreating to the kitchen to prepare dinner.

Mattie, stunned by her outburst, was speechless as well. She felt too humiliated to face Jonathan again, so she stayed alone in the room, lying in her bunk surveying what she had done.

The last rays of the sun poured through the window, casting a light on the crumpled papers, disheveled books, broken glass and dented cans. Mattie watched as one final sliver threw an accusing ray across the blue-blotched canvas in the corner, then all was darkness.

Still lost in black thoughts, she barely heard her father's insistent pounding on the latched door. She didn't answer. She refused to go to dinner or offer any explanation for the locked door.

By nine o'clock, a conversation outside the door told her that Mr. Cosgrave had given up hope of getting her to come out; he was suggesting that Jonathon sleep on the sofa. Jono agreed gladly, saying he never wanted to enter "that pig's pen" again.

Mattie went on brooding until she finally came to a decision. She couldn't slink around in the dark forever. She'd made a mess of things, but hiding wouldn't help. It was now painfully clear that her detecting days were over. Yet unlike Sherlock Holmes in "His Last Bow" or Hercule Poirot in *Curtain*, she'd ended a failure. What's more, she'd have to admit everything to her father, which wouldn't be easy. Jono'd probably spilled everything by now, anyway, peppering his tale with lurid descriptions of her fiendish behavior. She'd better get her version in fast, before Dad had her shipped to an asylum!

Reluctantly, Mattie finally climbed down from her bunk, unlatched the door, and headed for her father's study.

"Dad, can I talk to you?" she asked nervously. "I've a confession to make."

Half an hour later, the entire truth had been told.

Mattie considered omitting embarrassing details, then decided to confess all, unable to lie any longer. She described her class trip to the museum, trailing Mr. Milich, making a fool of herself in the public baths, the exploding biscuits, the goofy wig and playing hooky. She concluded with the gory description of the destruction of her room.

Mr. Cosgrave listened in grave silence.

"Well, that's all of it," she sighed, somewhat relieved.

"Not quite," he added sternly. "You omitted leaving me crazy with worry, wondering what was going on in your locked room all night."

"Gee I'm sorry, Dad. I couldn't face you at first."

"All right, Matilda, I won't lecture you. You already know all the dangers you might've gotten into. And I won't punish you either until I've reasoned out a proper one. Mainly, I'm glad it's finally off your chest. I've been sitting here all night wondering when you'd get around to telling me about it."

"Yeah, I figured Jono'd already snitched about the room."

"That's not what I meant," he added. "I was referring to the rest of it."

Mattie stared at her father. "You *knew* the rest of it? That's impossible!"

"Well only partly," he explained. "And that I just learned this evening. Your teacher Mrs. Almquist called. She mentioned that you hadn't submitted your composition about going to the Brooklyn Museum last Friday. She felt since you were home sick, you could catch up and not lose your grade."

"Wow," she gulped, "like Jono loves to say . . . Oh, what a tangled web we weave . . ."

"Jonathon's what I want to discuss," said her father. "I understand your secrecy about a hot case, though that doesn't justify it. But why get so mad at your brother? He wasn't involved. He's got so many projects of his own, he hasn't had time—"

"That's just it," Mattie interrupted. "Jono's precious projects! *He* caused the fight. I warned him to leave me alone, but he wouldn't stop bragging. He kept babbling about his crazy new plan to buy paintings and operate fancy hotels. Then he had the nerve to offer me a job as *house detective*. A deliberate put-down, and he knew it!"

"I see," said Mr. Cosgrave. "And you don't think Jonathon has the right to make plans, too?"

"Maybe so. But why does he always have to outdo me on everything? It's bad enough being a failure without his rubbing it in."

"Sounds to me as if you're mad at yourself, not Jonathon," her father observed.

"Sure I'm mad," she confessed. "Why shouldn't I be? *Nothing* turned out right. I was the big super-sleuth who knew so much about people. Well, I'm through with it all for good!"

"Don't be so negative, Mattie. One mistake doesn't

make you a failure. Maybe you were trying too hard."

"Females *have* to try harder," she argued, "especially if they want to do things better than men."

"Is that the point of Women's Liberation?" asked Mr. Cosgrave. "We're different but equal, isn't that the idea? I bet if you eased up on yourself a bit, you'd find your instincts more accurate than you think."

"Oh, Dad," she sighed, "you don't understand."

"Maybe not," he agreed. "But I know one thing. Putting yourself down won't help. Before taking on any more cases, you ought to solve your *own* problems."

"If only I hadn't been so wrong about Mr. Milich," she groaned. "That's what I can't understand. I was certain I'd seen him before."

Shrugging his shoulders philosophically, Mr. Cosgrave returned to his desk. "You obviously need time to sort things out. A good night's sleep might help."

"No, I can't go to bed yet," she said, pacing nervously. "I've been alone in that room too long already. Can't I hang around here awhile?"

"Suit yourself," he said, going back to his work.

Of all the rooms in the apartment, Mattie loved her father's study best. Filled with the clutter of his years as a journalist, it had the musty odor of old books and pipe tobacco. Often, she'd come in here when she wanted some privacy. She'd spend time browsing through Dad's bookshelves or looking at his pictures. An entire wall was filled with photographs from news stories he'd especially admired through the years.

As Mattie relaxed in the leather chair beside her father's desk, she found herself staring at one particular snapshot. It was of a group of men, their faces like death masks, peering from behind barbed wire. The instant Mattie saw it, a chill of recognition ran through her. "That picture," she said. "That's the one."

Mr. Cosgrave looked up from his work and glanced at the snapshot. "Not a pretty sight, is it?" he said. "But it's something we shouldn't forget. Some of the things they found in Dachau after the war were too brutal to record. That picture was taken the day they moved into the concentration camp. Those men were the lucky ones."

Mattie took a closer look at the snapshot. At last she knew why she'd recognized the fearful expression on Mr. Milich's face. It was mirrored in the eyes of each man in the picture. Though some were old and some young, all their eyes were similar.

"Gosh, Daddy," she said. "It's *awful*."

"Yes," he agreed. "But that picture's been hanging there for years. Surely, you've seen it before."

"I have," she said, "but I'd forgotten. Oh, poor Mr. Milich! *He* was in one of those concentration camps."

"How terrible. You didn't mention that."

"No, he didn't tell me," said Mattie, "but I know it's true. He has that same terrible expression in his eyes. I *knew* I'd seen it before."

"Well," sighed Mr. Cosgrave, "horrors like that can't ever be forgotten."

"But I thought he was a *criminal*. How could I have made such an awful mistake!"

"*Was* it a mistake?" asked her father. "You saw *fear* in Mr. Milich's eyes, and you were sensitive enough to notice."

"Oh, Daddy," she said, "I'm so mixed-up, about *everything*."

Mr. Cosgrave leaned over and kissed her cheek. "Don't worry so much," he said. "You've got a sensible head on your shoulders, Mattie, and a goodness inside. Once you realize that, things won't seem so bad."

CHAPTER

12

Mattie's talk with her father hadn't solved anything. He hadn't even given her a punishment. Returning to her room, Mattie found her pad and wrote the composition she owed Mrs. Almquist. After transferring many of her feelings to paper, her head seemed clearer.

Then determined to make amends to Jonathon, she compiled a list of self-imposed duties for the following day, set her alarm and went to bed. At six o'clock, she tiptoed into the kitchen and went to work.

When Jonathon came out to start breakfast, Mattie had already set the table, started the coffee brewing, poured the waffle batter and scrambled the eggs.

"What're *you* doing up?" he asked icily. "Planning to poison me?"

"It's part of my apology," she explained. "Relax and take the morning off."

"Oh?" he asked suspiciously. "Don't think you'll get off that easy. I've got fifteen dollars invested in that painting you ruined. If Mrs. Remington finds out—"

"Don't worry, I'll fix everything. There's a recipe for cleaning paintings in one of those art books. After school, I'll fix the room and clean off your precious picture."

Jonathon stared distrustfully. "What's the gimmick?"

Mattie's resolve to be nice was slipping. "I just told you, dum-dum. I'm trying to apologize. I acted awful yesterday, and I want to make it up."

"Well," he said, weakening, "I still haven't heard you *say* it."

Through a strained smile, Mattie tried sounding sweet. "I'm sorry, brother dear. I've been a beast."

"A *monster!*"

"That's right," she agreed, gritting her teeth. "A monster. And I promise never to do such a dreadful thing again."

"Well, all right," he said, "but don't forget to fix my painting. And those waffles better taste terrific."

Mrs. Almquist was quite impressed with the composition Mattie handed in that morning. After lunch, she read it aloud to the entire class. Besides recounting the classes' adventure in the museum, Mattie described the sad old man she'd met there and explained how badly she'd wanted to solve the art theft. She even confessed to her failure, finishing with these closing sentences: "So you see, I didn't solve the crime. But Mr. Milich said we must all look for good in everything. Sometimes we can't see it at first, but it's there. So, I think that meeting Mr. Milich was the good part of my experience at the Brooklyn Museum."

When Mrs. Almquist had finished, lots of kids groaned and shouted "corny," but not Melissa. She stopped Mattie after school and complimented her.

"Gosh, you were brave to confess defeat to the whole class," she said admiringly. And the way you told about that poor old man. I may've misjudged you, Matilda. You *do* have a sensitive soul!"

Mattie smiled and shrugged. Well, maybe even Melissa Remington was *human*!

Mattie returned home, determined to tackle her second chore, the one she really dreaded. Glancing around her room at the debris, she wondered if it could ever be put right. She began by replacing papers in files, picking up overturned books and bottles and straightening shelves. She threw out the broken test tubes and ripped folders, tacked up the oil cloth and swept the floor. But Mrs. Remington's painting was the biggest disaster of all. That dark blue ink splotch covered the entire upper corner. If she couldn't clean it, she'd owe Jono fifteen dollars.

Leafing through her art book, she came upon the recipe for cleaning paintings: a solution of baking soda applied with a hard tooth brush followed by alcohol lightly rubbed on with a cotton swab. Getting the ingredients from the kitchen, she set to work. The process was slow, but after a half-hour, she'd managed to clean away some part of the stain.

As Jonathon passed the room pulling his shopping cart, he stopped to see how she was coming. "Better get it all off," he threatened, "or you'll owe me—"

"Fifteen bucks, I know."

"I'm going shopping. Need anything?"

"Yeah, a pound of baking soda and a gallon of alcohol!"

"I'm not dragging that junk for you," he protested. "If you hadn't gone beserk and wrecked everything . . ."

"Okay," said Mattie, "I promised to put things right, and I will. I'll come and push the cart."

Grabbing her sweater, she followed Jonathon from the room. As Mattie was locking the front door, she noticed someone running into the elevator. She dashed down the hall, yelling to hold it, but it'd already gone.

"Some people have no manners," she puffed.

"You should talk," Jonathon grumbled.

As further penance for her sins, Mattie vowed to be as pleasant as possible in the supermarket. But it took all her patience to keep from socking Jono in the mouth. He was unbearable. Buying food, for him, wasn't a job, it was a *ritual*! He had to thump every melon, squeeze each tomato, pinch the peaches and sniff the cheeses.

A half-hour later, only halfway through the shopping list, Mattie was bored to distraction. She stood in the center aisle leaning on her cart, staring aimlessly out the supermarket window. Suddenly, she noticed someone outside staring back, a familiar face.

"Strawberry or vanilla?" asked Jonathon.

"What?"

"Which ice cream for dessert?"

"Have a heart, Jono. Hurry it up."

"But I don't know. Daddy likes strawberry best, but it's imitation flavor. Hey, lemon meringue pie's on sale. Bet it doesn't have real egg whites, though."

Mattie groaned and prayed for deliverance. Glancing toward the window again, the familiar face was gone. When Jonathon finally finished, like a dutiful sister, she lugged the shopping cart home. After dinner, she even volunteered to do the dishes. Mattie could see from Jono's confused expression, he hadn't a clue as to how long her guilt-ridden charity might go on. But he planned to make the most of it.

As Mattie scrubbed the last pot clean, Mr. Cosgrave came into the kitchen. "You're looking more chipper tonight."

"Yeah, Dad, you know the old saying—penance is

good for the soul. Since you couldn't think of a punishment, I made my own—being *nice* to Jonathon."

"And is that so hard?"

"Well," she groaned. "It isn't *easy*. You should've seen him in the supermarket today. Unbelievable!" After Mattie finished scrubbing the pot, she gazed at her reflection in its sparkling bottom. "Wow, did I make that shine, just like on TV," she said proudly. "Maybe I'll become a creative home engineer, too. Then Jono can compete with me for a change."

"Now Mattie," her father said, frowning. "I hoped you learned something from our talk."

"Just joking, Dad."

"Have you gotten around to fixing up your room? I hope that's part of your 'niceness' plan."

"Yeah! I swept up all my detecting equipment and dumped it in the trash."

Mr. Cosgrave looked surprised. "I didn't suggest you do *that*."

"Oh, it's okay," she added. "I'm finished with crime."

Her father seemed skeptical. "There's another old saying, you know. Leopards can't change their spots."

Once Mattie had put the kitchen in order, she went back to the job of cleaning the painting. Working with a toothbrush seemed to take forever, and she was still scrubbing long after Jonathon had gone to bed. As she progressed, Mattie noticed some oil paint beginning to lift off along with the ink. Startled at first, she carefully began scrubbing the spot. On closer observation, she noticed something she hadn't seen before. Now, she began scrubbing harder.

"It's past midnight," scolded her father as he passed the doorway. "Turn that lamp off and get in bed."

"Can't stop now," she protested, still scrubbing feverishly. "I'm getting fantastic results."

"They'll have to wait. You've got a rough day ahead tomorrow. It's dentist time, remember?"

"Oh no," she groaned. "This is more important. I've got to finish so I'll—"

"Matilda, don't argue. I'm taking off work early to meet you after school. You children need that check-up."

"But Dad, you don't understand."

"Good night," he said, switching off her light.

Knowing she was in enough trouble with her father, Mattie reluctantly said good night. But she couldn't sleep. Varied thoughts and images seemed to fill the darkness—snatches of ideas were finally beginning to piece themselves together.

Switching on her light, Mattie grabbed one of the art books from the foot of her bed. "Just as I thought," she mumbled, leafing through it. "It all makes sense now."

Careful not to wake Jonathon, she tiptoed down from her bunk and grabbed something from the corner. After a quick trip to the kitchen, she returned to bed where she finally fell asleep.

CHAPTER

13

The next afternoon, Mr. Cosgrave was waiting outside school for both Mattie and Jonathon.

At the dentist's office, they got their usual lecture on proper flossing methods and the evils of refined sugar, which they, as usual, ignored. Luckily, the dentist found no cavities, so their father's usual lecture on the sins of snacking was avoided.

Instead, as a surprise treat, Mr. Cosgrave took them out for dinner. They went to a French restaurant, where Jonathon ordered boeuf Bourguignon and onion soup. Mattie disgraced both her brother and the waiter by asking for a cheeseburger! Jonathon laughed about that all the way home. He was still cackling when Mr. Cosgrave unlocked the front door.

"You've no couth, Mattie. Gaston's chef spent hours preparing his succulent sauces, and you'd rather eat at MacDonalds."

"What's it matter?" she argued. "All turns to the same thing in the end."

"That's enough, kids," said Mr. Cosgrave, pushing open the front door.

As he switched on the light, the three of them stood in the doorway, staring into the apartment in disbelief. The place was a shambles! Furniture was knocked over, drapes were pulled down, pillows ripped open, drawers overturned. The potted plants by the window had been smashed, lamps broken, sofa cushions pulled apart.

"Good grief, we've had burglars!" said Mr. Cosgrave.

He ran to the study, Mattie and Jonathon quickly following. Their father's desk had been ransacked, his notes and files scattered all around. In the children's room, all the tidying up Mattie had done had been undone. In Mr. Cosgrave's bedroom, sheets and blankets were scattered about and pillow feathers swirled through the room, caught by the breezes from the opened window.

"They must've come in through the fire escape," he explained, glancing out the window. "Nobody out there now."

"Gee Daddy," said Jonathon. "What'd they take?"

"Look around and see, son. The police will want a list of stolen property."

Mr. Cosgrave checked through his study, while Jonathon surveyed the living room, and Mattie toured the kitchen.

"Our TV's still here, and so's the silverware," said Jonathon with relief. "And they didn't take our tape recorder or radio, either."

"My study's a mess," said Mr. Cosgrave, "but I can't find anything missing."

Jonathon rechecked the room. "Our household money's still inside the vase. A few dishes are broken, but all the crystal's here."

"No clothes are missing from the closets," said Mr. Cosgrave. "Thank God they didn't take your mother's old jewelry box. Those things are for Mattie when she's older. I don't get it! Someone smashed up our entire place, then left without taking anything. What were they *looking* for?"

"Beats me," said Jonathon, picking up a chair to sit on.

"*I* know what they were after," said Mattie coming from the kitchen, carrying a shopping bag. "But they didn't get it. I was too smart!"

Mr. Cosgrave glanced at his daughter. "What do you know about this, Matilda?"

"*Everything*, Dad," she said excitedly. "Of course, I didn't know I knew. But now I know what I thought I knew before. But I don't have time to explain." She ran toward the window and peered into the street. "I'll bet the front of the house is covered," she whispered.

As Jonathon and Mr. Cosgrave stared blankly, Mattie hurried into her room, kicking through the piles of debris until she came upon her deerstalker. She brushed it off and put it on. "Guess I'm not through with you, after all," she said. Fumbling through the overturned drawers, she found a role of Scotch tape. Then she ran into the bathroom and grabbed a can of talcum powder. Returning to the living room, she poured the powder on all the furniture.

"That's just great!" groaned Jonathon. "This place isn't messy enough!"

"Shut up," she ordered, busily sticking strips of tape on all the powdered surfaces. She picked each strip up, then held it carefully to the light until she'd found what she'd been looking for. "Okay Dad," she said, "we can go now."

"What are you *talking* about?" asked her father. "If you know anything, let's call the police and get to the bottom of this."

"Not now," she protested. "Besides, our local precinct can't handle this. We need a specialist."

Mattie hurried into the bedroom, her father following.

"We'll have to make a run for it down the fire escape," she said. "The front of the building might still be covered."

"I'm not running anywhere, Matilda. I want to know what's going on."

"Trust me, Dad," she pleaded. "I know what I'm doing. If I'm wrong, I'll clean up this whole mess by myself."

"Hey, that's a deal," said Jonathon. "Let's go."

Mattie quickly climbed out the window. "Grab that shopping bag, Dad. We've got to hurry."

"Matilda, this is ridiculous."

"Please, Dad. *C'mon.*"

Reluctantly, Mr. Cosgrave picked up the bulging bag and followed Mattie and Jonathon onto the fire escape. The corner lamppost glowed, lighting their way down the iron stairs. Turning the corner toward the next flight, Mr. Cosgrave glanced into the shopping bag. Startled at the contents, he shouted, causing Jonathon to slip a rung.

"Matilda Cosgrave, there's a *turkey* in this bag!"

"I know, Dad," she whispered. "Trust me!"

CHAPTER

14

Mattie's mind was jumping, her heart thumping, just like the good old days before she had given up detecting.

With Mr. Cosgrove still protesting loudly, she ran up the darkened side street. Approaching Broadway, she quickly hailed a cab.

"Where to?" asked the driver, throwing open the door.

"One Police Plaza," she said, scooting inside. "That's down in Wall Street, near the Brooklyn Bridge."

"One minute," Mr. Cosgrave insisted, pulling Jonathon back by the collar. He dropped the shopping bag to the ground. "I'm not paying a cab fare to take this turkey that far!"

"You've got to," Mattie urged. "Take that bag and get in."

The driver gave them all a peculiar glance as they settled into the cab.

"I think I've cracked the case, Dad," she said excitedly. "But I can't be certain until this turkey's been checked out."

"But Mattie, I thought you'd retired."

"Oh Dad, you were right about leopards. Mr. Milich was right, too. Good can be found in everything. All the clues were there, but I was following the wrong scent."

"Matilda, if you don't start explaining . . ."

"Okay," she said, "my big break came when I threw that inkwell at Jono's painting. Otherwise, I never would've known. When I started to clean away the ink, I noticed something strange. The upper right-hand corner with Adrian's signature had been painted over. In cleaning it, some of that paint came off. Remember my saying it could take years for oils to dry? Well, this paint was still wet. Underneath Adrian's signature, there was another one. I didn't have time to clean it all, but the last three letters are G-A-S."

"So what?" said Jonathon. "That spells *gas*.

"Or *Degas*," said Mattie.

"*My* painting?" he asked. "A real Degas?"

"*Is* it really your painting, brother dear?" she asked coolly. "Or another of your *secrets*. That's not the painting Adrian sold you, and you know it."

Jonathon sat in awkward silence.

"What's Adrian got to do with this?" asked Mr. Cosgrave.

"Everything," said Mattie. "He's not only a faker, but a *thief*. A smart one, too. He stole the Degas from the museum, then planned to pass it to a buyer that day at the fair. He stuck it in with all his phonies, so no one would suspect. Wow, what a perfect cover. Forgers pretend fakes are real. But Adrian pretended a priceless painting was a *fake*. Brilliant!"

"That doesn't make sense," said Mr. Cosgrave. "*Anyone* could've bought that picture. In fact, Jonathon did. From what you said, they all looked alike."

"With one exception," Mattie corrected. "This painting had a SOLD sticker on it. That sticker was Adrian's way of identifying the original. He thought he'd sold Jono a fake, but Jonathon switched the paintings. He took the SOLD sticker from the one he liked and stuck it on the one he didn't."

"Is that true, son?"

"Well," he stammered, squirming in his seat, "it was *prettier*. The colors matched Mrs. Remington's room better. I didn't think it mattered. They were all the same."

"See, Dad," Mattie continued. "That was the buyer's way of identifying the real Degas. Adrian must've told him to look for the SOLD sticker. Naturally, when he discovered it was a phoney, Adrian tried getting the real painting back. He'd noticed Jonathon admiring it. He's a smart guy, so it probably didn't take him long to figure things out. When I interviewed him, I told him your name and where you worked. That's how he discovered where we lived. Jono, remember the person who dashed out of the elevator yesterday as we were leaving? That was Adrian, staking out the house. He followed us to the grocery store, too. That's who I saw staring at me from the street. Then tonight, when he found we weren't home, he broke into the apartment, hoping to find the Degas. But I was too smart for him. Last night, I pieced the puzzle together. Once I realized that we might have the original, I found a hiding place till I could be certain."

Jonathon peeked into the shopping bag. "So you stuffed it in the turkey." He giggled. "But that was *my* idea."

"And a good one, too," said Mattie. "Adrian pulled our place apart, but never thought of checking the refrigerator. Last night, I took the turkey out of the freezer and stuffed the painting inside. Then I replaced it in the bottom of the refrigerator. Freezing it again might've cracked the oil paint."

Mr. Cosgrave sighed. "I guess it all makes sense in a crazy sort of way. But it's all guesswork, Matilda. You have no real proof."

"But I do," she argued. She opened her purse and

removed the strip of scotch tape from her notebook. "A perfect set of fingerprints," she said proudly. "This is the positive proof that will nail Adrian to the scene of the burglary."

"Well done, Matilda." Her father smiled. "But now, will you please tell me where we're going? This evidence should be taken to the police immediately. We can't ride around in a taxi with this turkey all night."

"We are going to the police, Dad. We're taking our turkey to the one man in the police department who can help us. Robert Volpe. I read all about him in a book called *The Art Cop*. Mr. Volpe runs the ART Squad, a one-man Art Recovery Team: the only one in the country. He works with galleries, museums, Interpol, the FBI and handles hundreds of art theft cases every year."

"I bet he's never worked with a turkey before," said Jonathon, laughing.

"That's because he's never worked with Matilda before," said Mr. Cosgrave. "I hope he's prepared for the experience!"

CHAPTER

15

Number One Police Plaza was a large building at the base of the Brooklyn Bridge. Mattie clutched her shopping bag tightly as they entered the lobby and approached the desk sergeant.

Dramatically, she dropped the shopping bag on his desk. "We've got to see Mr. Volpe right away. It's urgent."

"It's a theft," Mr. Cosgrave explained.

"You folks've got the wrong place," he said. "This is a special investigations unit. We're the Property Recovery Squad, but we don't handle stolen turkeys."

"It's not the turkey," she explained, "it's the *stuffing*. Mr. Volpe's got to see us."

"Perhaps we'd better come back in the morning," said her father. "Mr. Volpe probably isn't in this late."

"Oh, he's in," said the Sargeant. "If he's handling a big case, most times he's on twenty-four-hour call. I saw him go up awhile ago."

"Then can we see him, *please*," Mattie pleaded.

"Okay," he shrugged, glancing at the turkey. "Guess Bob's handled stranger things. You'll find him on the eleventh floor."

The Cosgraves took the elevator upstairs, then walked down a long hallway, past several departments, until they found Mr. Volpe's office. A large crest in the shape of a painter's pallette was stenciled on the door: N.Y.P.D.—A.R.T. SQUAD. Inside the small office, an oil painting of a seascape hung above the desk, with the signature, Volpe. A handsome young man with wavy brown hair and a trimmed, turned moustache sat behind the desk, checking through a large stack of files. He was dressed in a black pinstripe suit and vest. "Bob Volpe," he said, extending his hand. "How can I help you?"

"Wait a minute," said Jonathon suspiciously. "Are you sure this guy's genuine? He's not like cops I've seen. He's got no uniform or gun."

Mr. Volpe smiled. "Art recovery's a special line of police work, son. Luckily, we don't need guns."

Mattie's father shook hands and introduced himself. "I'm Mathew Cosgrave. These are my children, Jonathon and Matilda."

"And this is the turkey," said Mattie proudly, plunking it down on the desk. "I think it cracks the case."

"It must seem odd, our coming in here with a turkey, Mr. Volpe, but my daughter insists there's a stolen Degas inside."

"A Degas?" he asked with interest. "The Brooklyn Museum's Degas?"

"That's the one," said Mattie. "I rolled it up and put it in there myself. I'm a detective, too."

"This may seem hard to believe," said Mr. Cosgrave. "Mattie explained it all to me, but it still sounds ridiculous."

Mr. Volpe laughed. "Mr. Cosgrave, I've recovered priceless paintings from lockers in Grand Central Station, empty warehouses, and construction sites. Once I rescued thirteen Tiffany lamps from the Sanitation Department minutes before a garbage truck would have crunched them to bits. So if your daughter thinks there's a Degas in her turkey, I'd like to have a look!"

Mr. Volpe removed the turkey from the bag, pulling the rolled-up canvas out of the end. "Even before I look at this, I can tell you know something about art," he said. "You've rolled this canvas with the paint to the outside. Most people think rolling the other way is best, but that damages the piece."

"I know." She beamed. "I read that in a book."

"Let's see what else you know," he added with interest. Stretching out the painting, he held it to the light for examination. "It's the right size and the colors look authentic. But I see there's been some over-painting. Hey, what's this splotch in the corner?"

"That's where Mattie threw the inkwell," said Jonathon. "Right after her attack."

"Jono, shut up. Mr. Volpe, I threw that ink *before* I knew it was the Degas. I found out while I was cleaning it."

"Where'd you get this painting, Mattie?"

"Jono bought it at an art fair, from Adrian the art faker. But I've been handling this theft from the beginning. I was in the museum the day this picture was stolen! I've been following up leads ever since."

"*You've* been handling this case?" he asked in surprise. "I thought *I* was the only one."

"Mattie, you'd better give Mr. Volpe all the details," said Mr. Cosgrave.

Mr. Volpe pulled up some chairs, and Mattie recounted her entire adventure. He listened intently, occasionally responding with an impish grin.

"So you see," she concluded, "if Jono hadn't switched the paintings, I never would've known."

"The colors were so much prettier," Jonathon explained. "But I never thought Adrian would notice."

"An art lover, eh, Jonathon?" asked Mr. Volpe. "Me, too!"

"What do you say?" asked Mattie eagerly. "Is it the real thing? Can you arrest Adrian?"

"Well, Mattie, art theft's a hard thing to prove. Our main interest is recovering pieces intact. If the painting's genuine, the best we can hope for is a charge of criminal possession. Though we might get him on Burglary Two. Breaking into a house at night's a felony, carrying up to seven years. But we'd need proof of that."

"I've got proof!" said Mattie, handing her strip of Scotch tape to Mr. Volpe.

"This is a perfect set of prints," he said approvingly. "You really *are* a sleuth, Mattie. What do you say I take this Degas to a lab right now?"

"Oh, please, Mr. Volpe," Mattie coaxed, "may we come along?"

"Why sure," he said. "In this case, a simple X-ray's probably all that's necessary. But you can go if you like. I'll call the Metropolitan Museum and try to make arrangements."

"The Metropolitan!" shouted Jonathon. "Wow, I've never been there at night with no guards around. We can look at everything in private. Touch the stuff, too, maybe. Guards never let you touch. I've always wanted to feel the weight of some of those tapestries."

Mattie sneered. "We're not going there to feel tapestries, dodo. This is a scientific investigation."

"Then you really think the painting's genuine?" asked Mr. Cosgrave.

"Sounds nuts, eh?" said Mr. Volpe. "But I'll tell you, art thieves are a separate breed. I worked undercover narcotics for eight years and know the difference. People committing art fraud and theft don't even consider themselves in the same league. They like to do things with style—cat-and-mouse it. Mattie's story might seem wild, but it makes perfect sense."

"Well, I still can't believe it," said Jonathon. "It was pure luck we went to that street fair and bought this painting. Mattie's super sleuthing was all *accident*."

"Don't discount luck in crime detection," said Mr. Volpe. "Just last week I was at a cocktail party where I noticed a stolen painting on the wall. The hostess had no idea it was hot property. She'd bought it from a reputable dealer. He'd bought it from a gallery owner who'd bought it at auction. After a week of undercover work, I've just tracked it to its source. Good crime detection means making use of luck. Instincts, too."

"Right," Mattie agreed. "Jono doesn't understand about instincts, Mr. Volpe. He's not a detective like us. Listen, can we use the police siren on the way to the museum?"

"I don't think so, Mattie. Museums prefer discretion. Arriving with police sirens makes them nervous."

"Yeah, I get it," she said. "Undercover stuff!"

"That's right," he said. "Let's go."

CHAPTER

16

Minus the sirens, Bob Volpe's police car proceeded discreetly uptown. On arrival at the Metropolitan Museum, a man greeted them at the side entrance. He led them through the darkened empty halls and escorted them by elevator to the upstairs laboratories. There, they were met by an elderly man wearing a lab technician's smock and professorial-looking half-glasses.

Mr. Volpe shook hands. "Thanks for seeing us, Mr. VanVelden. I need a quick ID on a Degas."

"You're lucky to find us here," Mr. VanVelden explained. "We're all working late tonight. I've just received a shipment of Chinese bronzes the museum hopes to purchase."

"I *love* your Chinese bronzes," said Jonathon knowingly, "but you could use a few new ones."

"They don't want *new* ones," Mattie teased. "They want *old* ones, dummy. Going to check them out for fakes, huh?"

Mr. VanVelden peered over his glasses. "We prefer not to report an object as *fake*, young lady. We like to say it's been *misattributed*. Much more tactful."

Mr. VanVelden led them into a vast room, dotted with workbenches, items of equipment and works of art. Set in a corner was a lovely painted wooden statue of a woman in long flowing robes.

Jonathon noticed it immediately. "Gee, she's beautiful," he said. "I bet she's a princess."

"I like to think of her as a tree," said Mr. VanVelden. "And to determine her age, we have to discover when she was cut down. To learn when she stopped living, we'll run a carbon 14 test. All living things contain a small proportion of the radioactive isotope carbon 14. When they die, the carbon 14 begins to disintegrate at a constant rate. By determining how much still remains, an accurate date of death can be established. During the actual test, a tiny sample of this statue will be burned and reduced to carbon. The percent of carbon 14 present in the sample will indicate the age, or when the tree stopped living."

"Wow," said Mattie excitedly, "it's just like I read about. Forgers break their necks making things look scrungy, but they can't fool professionals! What are

you going to do on the Degas?"

"I'm taking it into the microscopy lab," said Mr. VanVelden, leading the way. He pointed out various devices: a metallurgical microscope with automatic camera, a micro-projector and a petrographic microscope used to study minerals.

"Is this where you're going to examine my painting?" asked Mattie eagerly. "We need scientific proof fast, before Adrian decides to split."

"You're right," Mr. Volpe agreed, unrolling the canvas and handing it to Mr. VanVelden.

The old man examined the surface silently for several moments. "Superficially, the canvas seems to conform to the period," he said, crossing the room and placing the painting on a table. "This is our twenty-power, long-arm binocular microscope," he explained, positioning it above a corner of the canvas. Then he bent over the eye pieces and twirled the focusing knob. "Looks credible, but there's been some repainting in this area."

"That's where Adrian stuck his signature," Mattie explained. "But Degas's name is underneath, see? When you tell us it's genuine, then we can nab the thief."

"Not so fast, young lady," said the old man. "Verification takes time. Let's go into the X-ray room."

Moving quickly, Mr. VanVelden put the picture on another table, switched off the overhead lights and flicked on an ultra-violet light. "See how the ultra-violet light makes that overpainted area jump out? That shows chemical changes between the original paint and the overpainting."

"That proves Adrian's been fooling around," said Mattie. "Is the painting underneath old?"

"I've not determined that yet," he continued. "First, it must undergo a series of photographs. It shouldn't take more than forty-five minutes."

"That long?" she asked impatiently. "I sure hope Adrian isn't *packing*."

The old man scurried around the lab, changing the lenses and filters on a bellows-type camera. He took color photos, then infra-red lamp photos, then ultra-violet light photos.

"Now," he explained, placing the picture vertically on a metal framework that hung against the wall, "our next step is X-ray." Aiming the camera at the canvas, Mr. VanVelden led everyone from the room. Closing the heavy lead-lined door behind him, they waited outside in a small X-ray control room. A master panel with dials and switches was against one wall and there was one tiny window. Through its thick leaded glass, Mattie could see back into the X-ray room. Her excitement grew, as she knew the painting would soon be verified.

Set into the wall beside the window was a fluoroscopic screen. Beneath that, two things that looked like machine gun grips stuck out from the wall. Mr. VanVelden grasped these and manipulated the buttons. There was a whirring noise. From inside the room, the painting glided up in front of the fluoroscopic screen and stopped. Mr. VanVelden pressed another button and a blurry image of a section appeared on the screen.

"This will show how the artist built up his paints," he explained. "Brushstrokes can tell us a lot about authenticity. I've seen X-rays of other Degas and know his technique."

"I know," Mattie agreed. "The way an artist lays on his paint is almost like a fingerprint."

"Exactly," he said. "Just one more test should do it. Let's take it to the spectroscopy lab."

In the next lab, Mr. VanVelden placed the painting under a laser microbeam probe. "When this beam hits the painting, it vaporizes a nearly invisible sample. This vapor is then exposed to the spectrograph, which analyses its chemical composition." Mr. VanVelden stared intently. "Very interesting," he said, finally. "I find no titanium in the white pigment."

"Then it's *genuine*," Mattie shouted. "I knew it!"

"How do you figure that?" asked Jonathon.

"Because, dear brother, *I'm* the art expert, not you. Titanium was first used in pigments in 1920. Degas died in 1917."

"Is that true, Mr. VanVelden?"

"Absolutely," he agreed. "If I were doing a report on this painting, I'd pronounce it an authentic Degas. Not one of his better pieces, but certainly genuine."

"At last!" shouted Mattie ecstatically, grabbing her father and whirling around the room.

"Of course," Mr. VanVelden added, "if the painting were of an older vintage, one final test would be necessary. Our X-ray non-dispersive analyzer converts electronic impulses, which are then transmitted into our computer. Numerically, it prints out the presence of zinc, cadmium and various other recent—"

"That's not necessary," said Mattie, "we're convinced."

"Yes," added Mr. Volpe. "Thanks so much for your time. Well, Mattie, I'd say you wrapped this case up. All that's left is to bring in your collar."

"Collar?"

"Adrian, your art faker," he explained. "When cops book a criminal, it's called a collar."

"Oh sure, I knew *that*."

"Let me drive you home," Mr. Volpe offered. "Then I'll file my report and track down Adrian. Better keep all this confidential until I've checked his prints and gotten him in custody."

"Oh, can't I come with you?" Mattie pleaded. "Catching the crook's the most exciting part. After all, he's my collar."

"I can't take that responsibility, Mattie. Adrian might try to resist arrest. It's no place for a child."

"I'm not a child, I'm a *detective*!"

"Yes," her father agreed, "and a terrific one, too. But it's past your bedtime. Thanks for all your help,

Mr. VanVelden. It's been very informative."

"It sure has," Jonathon added. "And mister, if you find that any of your bronzes are phoney, I've got a client who might want to buy one. Any one would look great on Mrs. Remington's coffee table!"

CHAPTER

17

It was past midnight when the Cosgraves arrived home. As a special reward for solving her case, Mattie was allowed to stay home from school the next day. Jonathon got the day off too, after he'd volunteered to clean the apartment.

When Mattie walked into the living room the next morning, Jonathon was busily puffing pillows and sweeping up broken crockery. She sat on the sofa and yawned. Already, the excitement of the night before seemed strangely distant, replaced by a peculiar emptiness.

"I made blueberry muffins," said Jonathon. "They're still warm."

"No thanks," she said. "I'm not hungry."

"I was starved this morning," he said brightly. "Excitement does that to me. Wasn't it fun last night, Mattie? I bet we're the only kids who've ever been inside the museum's lab. But I wish we'd been able to look at all those bronzes more carefully."

"Oh, Jono, all that dead junk!"

"Junk! I can't wait to tell Mrs. Remington I bought an original Degas for fifteen dollars. She'll *know* I'm a genius! But you know, you're not bad either, Mattie. How'd you know about that pigment stuff?"

"Good research is part of good crime detection," she said blandly.

"I guess there's more to it than I thought," he admitted. Jonathon interrupted his dusting long enough to glance her way. "But you don't look like someone who's solved a super crime. Don't you want to celebrate?"

"No," she said. "I'm not in the mood."

"When I'm a success, I always celebrate," said Jonathon. "But maybe girls are different; or detectives."

"I think I'll go for a walk," said Mattie, getting up and stretching. "Want to come along?"

"No chance," he said, rearranging the glasses in the china closet. "This clean-up'll take hours. That table needs polishing, Adrian's fingerprints are all over it. He messed up the plants, too. And look how he slashed those scatter pillows. I always hated them anyway. At last we can get new ones."

"Like Mr. Milich said," Mattie observed. "Good can be found in anything."

"Who?"

"Mr. Milich."

"Oh," nodded Jonathon, "that old guy." He scrubbed the last fingerprint from a china vase. "Well, maybe he's right."

Mattie got dressed, brushed her teeth and threw on her jacket. As she left the house, Jonathon was whistling happily, engrossed in the job of putting things in order. She hoped the fresh air would make her cheerful, too. She'd never felt so glum after a case before. Not only didn't she feel like celebrating, she barely felt successful. Things still had an unfinished feeling, like waiting for a second shoe to drop. Strange!

Mattie strolled along West End Avenue with no particular destination in mind. Finding herself on 99th Street, she turned down the corner and stopped outside a brownstone building in the center of the block. She'd passed it many times before and often read the brass plaque attached to the front door. Now, she suddenly realized something had drawn her there today.

Was this the missing link, the unfinished piece of the puzzle? Convinced it was, she walked up the stone steps and rang the bell.

Mattie spent over an hour inside the brownstone before her mission was complete. After that, she got on the subway heading toward Delancey Street. When she reached the rundown building and began to climb the stairs, she could hear the sound of the scratchy record playing inside. As she rang the bell, the record stopped. After a moment, the door chain was unlatched.

"Ah, my little friend," said the old man, both surprised and pleased. "What are you doing here?"

"Hello, Mr. Milich, may I come in?"

"Of course," he said, opening the door and ushering her into the living room.

The apartment was small, dark and sparsely furnished, but everything was neat and tidy. A clean linen cloth covered the table in the kitchenette, bookcases were filled with old, cracked leather volumes and many photographs in gilded frames were scattered around the room. A crank-up Victrola rested on a corner table beside a pile of old-style records, and lace curtains hung across the window.

"Come, sit down," he said, taking his jacket from the back of the kitchen chair and quickly putting it on. "I never thought to see you again. But I'm glad you're here. I was much concerned for you the other day. You are still in search of stolen property?"

"No, I've cracked the case," she said proudly.

Mr. Milich looked confused. "Ah, you mean you have solved the crime? Very good, little one. Oh, you must tell me all about it. But first, some refreshment." He hurried to the kitchen cabinet. "I'm afraid there is little," he apologized. "Just some camomile tea and biscuits."

"Oh, that's fine," said Mattie, "but don't bother."

"Is no bother. A friend comes to my door with good news, so we must be social, yes?"

Mattie watched as Mr. Milich puttered with the cups and saucers, arranging them neatly on a small silver tray. Then he placed the biscuits on a china dish. When the tea had brewed, he poured some into her cup. It smelled sweet and inviting.

"Now tell me, Mathilde," he said, seating himself across from her, "how did my little friend turn her defeat into victory?"

Mattie had never heard her name pronounced that way before—Ma-theeld—so old-fashioned and cozy, just like the sweet, hot tea and tidy little apartment.

"It was just like you said," she began. "A person should never give up. I only *thought* I was a failure."

Nibbling on her biscuits, Mattie eagerly began explaining the incidents of the previous day, ending with her trip to the microscopy laboratory of the museum.

Mr. Milich listened in rapt interest. "How clever of you," he said admiringly. "So this fellow Adrian was the culprit, yes? Poor man."

"Well, he wouldn't have been poor if he'd gotten away with it," said Mattie, gulping her tea.

"Is not what I mean, Mathilde. Money cannot bring richness of the soul. Such a man is poor to have so little faith in himself."

"Maybe so," she said. "Adrian said he started faking paintings because no one wanted his. I guess he was so jealous of those famous artists, he decided to steal their stuff."

"Ah, but some things cannot be stolen," Mr. Milich sighed. "Another's memories, experience, talent; these are his always. Perhaps with perseverance, Adrian too could have become a great artist. But one must *persevere*. Things of value do not come easily."

"I guess so," she agreed, "but it's hard to know what's really important. Sometimes, things turn out to be less than we expected."

Mr. Milich smiled knowingly. "You find your victory brings little pleasure, Mathilde?"

"Well, it wasn't the big deal I thought it'd be," she confessed. "I guess I was so anxious to impress Jonathon, I didn't think of much else."

"Jonathon?"

"My brother."

"Ah," he nodded, "but your brother, he is not impressed?"

"Hardly. Oh, this morning he finally admitted I'd been clever. For Jonathon, that's darn good! But something still bothered me, and I couldn't think what."

"Well," he suggested, "sometimes, is harder to please ourselves than others."

"Oh, I figured it out," Mattie continued. "It was you, Mr. Milich. *You* bothered me."

"I?" he asked, surprised. "Is not my wish to make concern for you, child."

"No," she explained, "I was *worried* about you. You seemed so lonely, and I felt guilty for suspecting such awful things; especially when I realized you'd been in a concentration camp."

Mr. Milich stiffened and his face grew white. "Such things I never speak of."

"I'm sorry," she said, "I didn't mean to blurt that out."

"But how did you know?" he asked. "I never mention this."

"You didn't have to," she explained. "I saw it in your eyes. My dad has a photograph of refugees from those camps. When I looked at those men's faces, I knew. It made me feel worse for ever suspecting you. I really didn't mean to remind you of it. I know it was a terrible thing, but my dad says none of us should ever forget it."

"Is true," the old man said. "None should forget. To forget would make it meaningless. Some of our people were destroyed not only by the gas, but by the fear within, which made them less than human, like their captors. But many found the moral energy to survive. And each one who survived became a testimony to the endurance of all men."

"But those awful years," said Mattie. "And your poor little girl."

"Still, one *must* go on," he said with resolve. "At

158

least my Vesna was spared the horrors of that place. Many children were not." Mr. Milich tried managing a smile. "You would like to see a picture of my Vesna?" he asked. Walking to the bookcase, he took a small gold frame from the shelf and handed it to Mattie.

The young girl in the photograph had long dark curls and an open, smiling face. Mattie felt strange, looking at a child who'd died long before she was born; to see in it a vague resemblance to herself. But it reminded her of someone else, too. "I know," she said, suddenly recognizing the similarity. "It looks like the portrait in the Brooklyn Museum. The little girl in the straw hat."

"Yes," agreed Mr. Milich. "That, too, reminds me of my Vesna. Often, I go to look at her. Though it was painted almost a hundred years ago, the artist captured universal childlike qualities. Such things never die; beauty lives, humanity endures. Can you understand such things, Mathilde?"

"Maybe so," said Mattie, glancing at the photo. "Yes, I think I do."

"I'm sure you do," he said, patting her hand. "You feel deeply and see much, little one. But enough of the past. You have come to share your victory with this old man, and I am grateful."

"No, I didn't come for that," said Mattie. "I came to help you, Mr. Milich. You and Dad were right about me, but I had to figure it out myself. I thought finding the crook was all I cared about. But that portrait in the museum, the photo in Dad's room, this picture of Vesna; those are important things, too. They're all connected in a funny way I don't understand."

"Is kind of you to worry for me," he sighed. "But there is nothing to be done."

"Oh, there is," she insisted. "I've discovered you don't have to be deported, like you thought. There's a place in my neighborhood called the Association for Yugoslav Jews in the United States. I stopped in there today and told them all about your problem. Yugoslavian immigration laws aren't as strict as other Iron Curtain countries. If you can support yourself and have a friend to vouch for you, your visa can be extended. You do have some money, don't you, Mr. Milich?"

"Money? Yes, enough."

"And your friend will vouch for you?"

"Jacob is a dear man. He much wants to help."

"Then you can stay indefinitely!"

"Is true?" he asked. "I do not have to leave this country?"

"That's right," said Mattie. "A nice lady at the Association explained everything to me. She says there are lots of cases like yours; old people with no relatives, scared of anything official. She explained how carrying visa cards reminds you of the awful days of Occupation. But they'll handle the details for you and help out if there's any problem. So you see, you can stay as long as you like."

Mr. Milich's eyes brightened. "To be given such a gift is a true kindness. But now, it is I who must feel sadly. For such an occasion, I should have a gift in return, but there is nothing. One cannot celebrate with tea and biscuits. In my country, good news requires a feast."

"That's funny," smiled Mattie, "suddenly I *do* feel like celebrating."

Mr. Milich stood up excitedly. "I will go now and bring back food for such a feast."

"Gee, no," said Mattie. "I can't stay."

"Of course," he said, appearing embarrassed, "perhaps you would rather not. You must go home."

"I know," she suggested. "You come home with me. I'm sure Dad would love to meet you. We could all have dinner together."

"I could not," he said. "You have done too much already."

"It'd be fun, really. And of course, you've got to meet Jonathon, too. When he's not being a pest, he's actually a darn good cook."

CHAPTER

18

With a bit more coaxing, Mattie managed to convince Mr. Milich he'd be a welcome guest. Once they'd arrived home, she proudly introduced him to her father.

"This is my good friend, Mr. Milich. I've asked him for dinner."

"Come in," he said warmly. "Mattie's told us about you."

"I hope Jono's fixed something really terrific," said Mattie. "I've been bragging about what a super cook he is."

"Jonathon's got the night off from kitchen duty," explained Mr. Cosgrave. "Another friend has arrived, and he's supplied us with a lovely dinner."

Mattie glanced around the living room, then noticed Mr. Volpe coming from the kitchen.

"Aha," he smiled. "Our super-sleuth returns! I brought your turkey back, Mattie. You left it in my office last night. Since I took your stuffing, my wife thought it only fair we replace it. Hope you like chestnut dressing."

"And it smells delicious," added Jonathon, grabbing the crystal salad bowl from the china closet. "I'm mixing up my special dressing for the salad. A perfect combination."

"Did you nab Adrian?" asked Mattie excitedly. "Did he confess? Did the prints match?"

"Yes to everything," said Bob Volpe. "Your fingerprints were positive proof. Adrian confessed taking the painting, but refused to divulge the prospective buyer. Thieves honor, you know. I did a make on him and found it's his first offense. Just got tired of selling cheap copies, I guess."

"Ta-DAH" Jonathon announced dramatically, carrying a huge tray toward the dining room. The turkey was roasted to a brown perfection!

"A masterpiece," announced Mr. Cosgrave.

"And wait till you see my salad," Jonathon added. "I had some mushrooms and fennel in the crisper. This is going to be a *feast!*"

When everyone was seated around the table, Mattie told of her trip to the Association and the good news she'd acquired for Mr. Milich. "So he doesn't have to leave the country, Dad, isn't that great?"

"I have only your daughter to thank for my good fortune," said Mr. Milich. "She has done me a great kindness."

"Yes," smiled Mr. Cosgrave. "Kindness is part of Mattie's nature. And if you need any further help, I'll be glad to vouch for you myself."

"You are too generous," he said. "Everyone. This delicious meal, your lovely home; such wonderful new friends."

"It's our pleasure," said Mr. Cosgrave. "After all, true happiness only comes through sharing."

"That's right," agreed Jonathon. "A gourmet meal's only appreciated if it's eaten."

"This salad's terrific," said Mattie. "Your dressing's great."

"It certainly is. I'm just sorry our celebration's based on someone else's misfortune," Mr. Cosgrave observed. "This Adrian fellow doesn't sound like a hardened criminal to me."

"He's not," Mr. Volpe agreed. "Being a struggling artist can be rough. I paint myself and know how frustrating it is. But he's a first offender, so the judge'll let him off easy. Still, it is all in the way you look at things. When a criminal steals a painting, he's stealing a part of history—all our history; it's irreplaceable. As you said, happiness comes from sharing, and the artwork in our museums is meant for everyone."

"Just so," agreed Mr. Milich. "During the war,

much art was sheltered from the enemy. One cannot put a money value on genius. The beauty great artists create must endure."

"Just like people?" asked Mattie.

"Yes," said Mr. Milich. "Just like people."

"Speaking of money value," added Mr. Volpe, "brings me to the subject of dessert."

"You brought that, too?" asked Jonathon.

"In a way. Our dinner's been so pleasant, I forgot I'd saved the best for last. When I returned the Degas to the museum this morning, the director was delighted. He told me there's a five thousand dollar reward for its recovery. Of course, it goes to you children."

"Five thousand dollars?" shrieked Jonathon.

"Five thousand bucks, that's fantastic!" Mattie shouted. "Think of all the stuff I can buy. I'll replace all my detecting equipment. New test tubes, new microscope . . ."

"New curtains and pillows for the living room," Jonathon shouted.

"And new bank accounts for your college educations," Mr. Cosgrave added.

"Wow, won't old Bascomb be surprised when she returns," Jonathon giggled. "She was afraid we couldn't live without her, and in just a few days, we've become *rich*!"

"She'll be surprised all right," said Mattie, "This turkey we've just eaten was Bascomb's prize possession. She's been saving it for *Thanksgiving*."

"Thanksgiving?" asked Mr. Milich. "Is that not an American holiday?"

"That's right," explained Mr. Cosgrave. "It began with some of the first people who came to this country. When they arrived, they were frightened and distrustful of others. But those they feared turned out to be friends. After hard work and understanding, they all set out a feast, sharing the rewards of their harvest."

"Aha," Mr. Milich nodded. "Well then, cannot we consider this our Thanksgiving?"

"Yes," said Mr. Cosgrave. "I guess we can!"

AUTHOR'S NOTE

The art detection laboratory described in this book is patterned after that of the Museum of Fine Arts in Boston, Mass. The Metropolitan Museum also has such a lab, though perhaps not quite as large.

Mr. Robert Volpe is the actual detective attached to the A.R.T. Squad in New York. Through his efforts, millions of dollars worth of stolen art has been recovered.

On Thursday, December 12, 1974, an art theft, similar to the one described in this book, occurred. A Renoir valued at fifty thousand dollars, entitled *Still Life With the Blue Cup*, was stolen from the Brooklyn Museum. Two hundred people were detained nearly two hours as museum officials locked all doors and the police searched all the visitors.

No ransom was ever demanded.

Nineteen months later on Wednesday, July 21, 1976, the Renoir was returned to the museum in the afternoon mail, undamaged. The package was wrapped in plain brown paper and addressed to the museum's director. The 16 inch by 13 inch oil had been carefully tucked in white tissue taped to a supporting board, inside a pillow case and a small plastic bag. After careful examination, the painting was found to be in perfect condition.

Scrawled in red ink on the inside of the outer brown wrapping was a crudely worded, unpunctuated, unsigned warning of future robberies at museums in the country. It said:

> *The museums in the U.S. need armed guards it wont be long before armed robbery's of art museums are happening believe me I know!*

The Brooklyn Museum
Bequest of Mrs. Laura B. Barnes